Donated by
Floyd Dickman

BACKSTAGE
PASS

BACKSTAGE PASS

Gaby Triana

HarperCollins*Publishers*

For Michael

Library of Congress Cataloging-in-Publication Data
Triana, Gaby.
Backstage pass / Gaby Triana.—1st ed.
p. cm.
Summary: After moving to Miami, Florida, sixteen-year-old Desert McGraw, whose life as
the daughter of a rock star has been anything but normal, determines to make a permanent
home for herself and her family—even if it means breaking up the band.
ISBN 0-06-056017-7 — ISBN 0-06-056018-5 (lib. bdg.)
[1. Rock music—Fiction. 2. Musicians—Fiction. 3. Fame—Fiction.
4. Interpersonal relations—Fiction. 5. Family problems—Fiction. 6. Moving,
Household—Fiction. 7. Miami (Fla.)—Fiction.] I. Title.
PZ7.T7334Bac 2004   2003019040
[Fic]—dc22   CIP
                                                                    AC

Typography by Larissa Lawrynenko
1 2 3 4 5 6 7 8 9 10

First Edition

Acknowledgments

Thanks to . . .

Oliver González for believing that I could.

Michael González for taking long naps that allowed me to write.

Steven Chudney for your great work, insight, and expertise. Oh yeah, and for getting me this gig!

Leann Heywood for being the coolest editor ever. You are a genius.

Joyce Sweeney for waving your magic wand over me. Look, I made it to the ball!

Yolanda Triana (a.k.a. Mom), **Oscar S. Triana** (a.k.a. Dad), **Oscar A. Triana** (a.k.a. Goober; thanks also for teaching me karate and judo), **Saundra Rubiera, Adrienne Sylver, Chris Núñez** (Hi, Guid!), **Devin Núñez, Marjetta Geerling, Danielle Joseph,** and **Fermin González** for taking the time to critique the whole first draft and not burst into tears of laughter! I appreciate it!

Thanks also to "Wednesday Nighters" who contributed wonderful ideas to this story—**Linda Rodriguez Bernfeld, Susan Shamon, Liz Trotta, Elaine Landau, Mari Locklin, Kim Moore, Sue Van Wassenhove, Marian Sneider,** and **Ruth Vander Zee**—as well as **Eduardo Figueredo, Isabel Avendaño, Joan Montoto Sánchez, Graciela Triana,** and **Brigette Triana,** for showing interest in my little story! Thank you!!!

And finally to the Purple Lady, **Nana,** for passing your love of language on to me. I miss you so much.

Chapter One

Day One. Let's see how long it takes before the madness begins. Because it will, you know. It always does. The fake smiles, the wannabe friends, the *can-you-get-me-backstage-passes?* I just got here and already I want this to be over with.

"Careful, okay?" Mom pulls to a stop at the corner of Palm Grove High.

Sigh. "Will you stop it?"

"Sorry, hon. Sorry." She glances around, looking for paparazzi that aren't there.

"Everything's going to be fine," I tell her. I know I need to watch my back, but it's not like *everyone* is out to get us. Nobody even knows I'm here, for Christ's sake.

"Desert, I was just wishing you luck, that's all," she says, pushing buttons on her cell, flinging back her tangled mess of brown hair.

"I know, Mom. See you later."

"Do I pick you up?"

"No, I'll walk."

She raises an eyebrow at me.

"I'll walk!" I repeat. "Now, go. Leave! Adios, ciao, buh-bye!"

She kisses her fingertip and touches my cheek right before I get out of the car. Then she's off, adjusting her earpiece, leaving me alone with this whole new school, whole new situation to deal with.

But I asked for it. To get away from my old life on the road, tour tutors, and recent death threats at St. Alphonsus—my last school in LA, and the one that I attended the longest. Cut short after three whole months. All because my dad said "pro-choice" in an interview with *Rolling Stone*. So freakin' what? No need to get testy, people.

So while the rest of the band is renting here in Miami during the recording, we're staying for good. I insisted on public school because I want to meet real kids for a change. At St. Alf's, everyone was just so ultrafake. This one's dad is a writer for *Newsweek*, this one's mom is a personal chef to the stars. How about a mother who types from nine to five in an office? Or a dad who cuts grass? That'd be so cool. So normal.

When I walk in the school's main office, some kid is on his way out. I recognize his T-shirt. On the front it says "Crossfire— Insanity Tour." Yep, I remember that tour well, having tagged along for six months. This is going to be way harder than I thought.

"Hi, I need my schedule please," I tell the front desk secretary.

"Name?" She looks about as friendly as an ice bucket.

"Desert McGraw."

"Desirée?" she winces, leaning her ear closer to me.

"Desert," I repeat. *Good Lord.* "Like the sandy place with the camels?" My parents should fry for naming me that. I mean, I was only a baby for crying out loud.

The secretary seems confused. "Oh," she says and types "McGraw" on her keyboard.

That's one good thing. Few people ever recognize my last name, because my dad only goes by one name—Flesh. Like Cher or Madonna, only a lot dumber. His real name is Richard.

"What grade?"

"Eleventh." I glance around and see a kid sitting in a chair, holding a bag of ice to his bruised temple. *Into a fight already, buddy?*

"One second, it's printing," Ms. Secretary says. Then she rips the sheet at the perforation and hands it to me.

Honors English Lit, first period. Cool, I can deal with that. English has always been my favorite subject. At least it's not physics or calculus. Honors English means you're a poet, a spirited soul, not some dorkus trying to come up with a way to clone superheroes in case we lose Spider-Man to Big-Boobed Evil Woman in Black.

I'll be late, though. Shoot. I hate walking in late to class.

English is in Room 214, second floor. I studied the map the night before, so I wouldn't look like a complete buffoon searching for my classes. When I get to the door, I hear the teacher already taking roll.

"Ow-ray-lee-o Gonzalez."

"Here."

Aurelio. Okay.

"Jesus Christian?"

"Here."

Jesus Christian? Holy . . . That's too funny!

She goes on while I slip in undetected and slide into the last desk in the second row. The girl next to me in the third row has a guitar. Not in a hard case, but in an old gig bag. Her eyes scan over my very normal and, might I add, very clever outfit—jeans and a T-shirt. Ha! Nobody will ever suspect me now!

"Nice shoes," she whispers.

I look down at my Prada platforms with the tan embroidered flowers. Damn, I knew I shouldn't have worn these. Dead give-away.

"Thanks," I say, glancing at her and trying really, really hard to find something about her ensemble worth praising. *Hmm* . . . no makeup, stringy hair, black baggy shirt and pants, rotting black sneakers. My eyes land on the floor. Her guitar case. "Cool gig bag."

Cool gig bag? At least I said something nice.

She turns her face to me and stares for a second. "Thanks. It was my mom's."

I smile. Whatever. It's not like I asked.

The teacher, who I figure is Ms. Smith judging from the SMI printed in the name column of my schedule, pauses in the roll taking.

"Desert . . . McGraw?" she says hesitantly.

"Here."

And the heads whip around, as usual, so that everyone can look at the freak show with the geological name. What are the chances that someone knows me? I smile a yes-may-I-help-you smile and the faces turn back around. Except for one. A real nice one with blue eyes. *Hoo!*

"Liam." Guitar Girl speaks again.

"Huh?"

"The guy looking at you. His name's Liam."

"Oh." I give Liam a quick glance, trying to take in as much as possible about him without staring. All I get in one and a half seconds is . . . brown hair . . . really cute . . . and . . . He faces the front of the class again. Bummer.

She flips a page in her notebook and begins doodling. "I'm just telling you 'cause I figure you don't know him."

"Why would you figure that? We might be great friends." I mean, *really*.

Then her pale green eyes—something so sad about them—are on me. "Everyone in this class was in the same Honors English last year. Except for you. So I'm sorry for assuming you're new." She glares at me for a split second before going back to her scribbling.

Okay, now I feel bad. Why am I being such a craphead? Didn't I say I wanted to meet real kids, and now I'm acting like a friend-repellant? "No," I say, pausing until she looks at me again. "I'm sorry. I'm just stressed out from moving, first day, new school."

"Moving from where?"

"LA."

"Wow. That's a big change. LA to Miami."

"Well, it may only be temporary, but so far I like it here."

"Ladies," the teacher calls from the front of the room. "We'll have plenty of time to get to know each other in just a moment. Could you please hold back on the chatter?"

Well! Aren't we quite the authoritarian?

"Sorry," Guitar Girl says aloud, then continues doodling.

"Ms. Smith" then smiles and introduces herself as Ms. Smigla. Imagine that, someone with a weirder name than me. She talks a *lot* and hands us our course outlines. After we review them and the books we're required to read this year, she actually gives us time to socialize! All teachers should strive to be so cool.

"So why'd you move from LA?" my nameless friend asks.

Let's see, I have lots of choices here. Do I say it's because I wanted a normal life away from cameras, reporters, and the red carpet? Or because a deranged fan-slash-classmate threatened to blow up our house if my dad didn't apologize to the pro-lifers who've always supported him?

Or the real reason, according to Dad? "We need a change, Desert, and Miami's the perfect place to record the new album. Energy, color, culture . . . just the essence our last album desperately needed." Essence, my butt. Personally, I think he just wants to veg on the beach. Why else would they have picked South Beach Sounds, a recording studio two steps from the sand?

"My dad had to relocate," I tell her. Yes, lies always work better.

"What does he do?" she pries.

Oh, whatever. Everyone's gonna find out eventually, anyway . . . but at least I'll have some time to fake normalcy until they do. "He's an artist," I say, playing with the zipper on my backpack.

"Cool. I'm Becca, by the way."

And she could care less! Excellent.

"Becca? Like Rebecca? I'm—"

"Desert. I know."

For a moment I stare at her. She knows everything. She's been playing me all along. She can see right through me and is about to tell me so. *Run, Desert! Get out while you still can!*

"Ms. Smigla called your name, remember?"

Oh. Doy. Living with a famous dad will do that to you. Sometimes I get paranoid. Just a little.

"You see that guy over there?" she asks, pointing to a decent-looking kid wearing a Dolphins jersey, number thirty-four, Williams. Seems harmless enough.

"Yeah?"

"His last name's Kuntz, so don't feel too bad about your name."

I think I spit my laughter into the hair of the guy in front of me. Becca lowers her forehead onto the desk and does everything in her power not to laugh out loud. Cool, I've met someone I can be friends with . . . well, maybe. Too soon to tell. When our giggles finally die out, Ms. Smigla announces the homework assignment and we copy it down.

"What other classes do you have?" Becca asks, looking over at my printout.

"Next one is physics," I say without much enthusiasm.

"Liam's in that one too, I think."

I guess she has a thing for Liam. "Want me to get his number for you?"

"No, I'm not into him," she says. "I've known him since fourth grade. He's like a brother to me. Trig with Ms. Gallo, awesome."

"What? Oh, we have third period together. Good, I guess I'll see you later then. Nice meeting you, Becca."

"Yeah, same here. By the way, I know you probably don't like your name, but I do. It's different. Your parents must be totally unique people."

"Thanks," I say with a smile. *That's only the tip of the iceberg as far as different, sweetie. If you only knew the rest.*

The bell rings, and thirty of us get up not a second too soon. Becca closes her notebook, and as she moves to put it away I spot them—her scribblings all over the front.

Crossfire Rules! Flesh is a god!!!

Wonderful.

Chapter Two

"Her Royal Highness has arrived!" My voice echoes throughout the empty house. I look at the boxes still lying around unpacked. Nobody answers, but I hear some laughing coming from the room my dad's been using as an informal studio. I throw my backpack onto the couch, walk through the living room, and open the door.

"Hey, girly!" Dad says when he sees me. I like his new casual look with the jeans and the buzz cut. The long hair just wasn't working anymore. Especially since his scalp shows more now than when he was twenty-five.

"Hey, Dad."

He's sitting with his acoustic guitar in front of a stack of sheet music, a sight I've known all my life. There's a girl no older than twenty-one opposite him, someone I recognize but can't pinpoint. She smiles at me.

"Des, this is Faith Adams, from The Madmen," he says. Oh. Right. I've never seen her in person, so I didn't recognize her without the clown makeup and freaky hairdos.

"Hey, I liked your video for 'Real.' It was cool," I tell her.

Actually, it sucked.

"Thanks," she says, and looks at my dad kind of funny. I don't know how to explain it. It's like she's sending him some sort of message and will probably tell him something about me when I leave the room.

So I walk in and make myself comfortable on the couch. "Where's Mom?"

Dad fingers a chord then points his pick behind him. "She's out back, getting sun, I think. How was school?"

I shrug and look at Faith. I don't know why it bothers me that she's here. I'm used to my dad working with different musicians and having them over, but it's usually other men. "It was okay, I guess. You've got fans there."

"Is that a bad thing? You say it like it is."

"No, of course not. It's just that I don't know how long I have before they find out, you know?"

"Well, they shouldn't find out. I don't think it's out yet that we're here, so you should be okay for a while."

"Hope so. There's a girl I met who seemed real nice, but now I don't think I can be friends with her."

"Why not?" Faith asks.

Who invited her into this conversation? I look at her long nails, obviously acrylic, since one of the pinky ones is missing, showing an ugly nail-bed. "'Cause she's a big-time fan. It's all over her notebook."

Dad presses his lips together and gives me a sympathetic look. I know he feels bad sometimes. Like he's putting me through something I don't want to go through. It *is* his fault, in a way, but I know there's not much he can do about it. Which is why I just try to deal with it the best I can.

"Well, how can anyone *not* be a fan of your dad's?" Faith asks, batting her eyelashes at him.

My jaw almost drops. What the hell is *that* supposed to mean? She must think I'm retarded to not see what she's doing. Why is Mom out back, anyway? Shouldn't she be in here making sure this tiger chick doesn't pounce on her man?

Dad is staring intently at his hands, forming one chord after another and humming quietly to himself. Good, he didn't even see the bait. Maybe Faith will realize he's not biting and give up fishing altogether.

I shoot her a look, the same one my mother gives the hard-bodies who line up backstage after each concert, and get up to leave.

"Love you, babe," Dad sings, and I know he's talking to me.

"Love you, Dad." He'll be fine. My dad doesn't ever seem to get distracted by all the women who sometimes surround him, but still it's annoying. I don't know how Mom deals with it.

The house is freezing. They must've turned the temperature down to like fifty or something. I open the French doors to the patio and feel the burning heat roast my eyes. Could Miami be any hotter?

My mother, Crossfire's manager from the very beginning, from even before she hooked up with Dad, is lounging on the deck, slathering sunscreen on her perfect skin. She's with Marie, her assistant for the last ten years. Assistant and friend. Marie's the one who makes calls, answers calls, denies, accepts interviews, etcetera. She also serves as my personal counselor sometimes, so I love her like a sister. Especially since I've got no siblings.

"Hey, Desi," Marie greets me with that pretty smile of hers. If she'd only lose like thirty pounds, she'd have any guy she wants.

"Hey, Babalú," I kid back. We've always done this *I Love Lucy* thing.

"Sweetie!" Mom cries. "How was school?"

Can parents ever think of anything else to ask when we come home from school? Did they forget the repetitive, brainless work, the incompetent teachers, the moronic kids who spend their precious energy trying to impress one another? Oh, wait. It *was* my first day.

"Hey, guess the good news," she says, totally forgetting the school question.

I lean over and kiss her cheek. "I dunno, Dad's getting a complete identity change, allowing us to roam Disney World freely without being recognized?"

And her eyebrow goes up.

I thought it was funny.

"Desert . . ." she says, like a reminder of everything we've ever talked about.

"Sorry. What? Tell me the good news already!"

"Faith Adams is working on some of the new songs for our next set!" she announces, as if this is supposed to be exciting.

"Why? What's wrong with Ryan?" Ryan's our current producer and big-time collaborator when it comes to lyrics. He's like a young grandpa to me. I don't want to lose a third grandpa.

"Nothing's wrong with Ryan, hon. It's just that we're trying to go with something a little more modern and, well, the last songs, as much as the critics liked them, didn't hit big with the twenty-five-and-under bracket."

And?

"But you can't pay attention to that. You have to do what you feel is right. Isn't that what you always said? And besides, if the twenty-five-and-under bracket didn't like the songs as much, then why'd we nab the Grammy?"

Mom and Marie exchange smirks like I obviously still have a lot to learn. "Do you really want to explore that one, Desert?"

"So Ryan's not going to work with us anymore?" *Because if he's not, I'm gonna throw myself on the floor and have a tantrum right here with those seagulls watching.*

"No, honey, we're not replacing him. We're just trying out new blood."

"But Mom, Faith's songs are all, 'Dance tonight, dance tonight, rock your body, feel all right.' That's crap."

"Desert, we're trying to come up with a more up-to-date sound. You know, to appeal to the younger crowd."

Great. I was hoping they wouldn't do this. I've seen it before. A twenty-year-old band, like Powerhouse, tries appealing to the younger crowd, and they suddenly look stupid. Forty-year-old rockers dying their thinning hair, trying to look cool for the kids. Why don't they just let the new bands take care of this? Crossfire has been around longer than I have—seventeen years. Their time is ending. Just let it be and accept it. But *nooo*.

"Isn't this risky?" I ask. "I mean, what if this brings bad reviews? Why can't we just stick to our sound, to what's worked in the past?"

"Desert, sometimes we have to take risks. How do we know what we're capable of if we don't try?"

She's right. She's always right, damn her. That's why I picked public school, to take a risk, try something new.

"Besides, we *are* sticking to our sound. It's just a few songs we're going to play around with. It's no big deal. I thought you'd be excited to have Faith around. She's the hottest thing right now, isn't she?"

I guess. Brianna, Marie's niece and my friend back in LA, likes her a lot.

"Yeah, she's way hot right now. Maybe you should go in there and cool her off." I turn and walk back toward the house.

"Desert, relax," my mom huffs.

I don't know what to make of all this. It's just that a new album means touring, and touring means we'll take off again. I've lived on and off the road my whole life and seen about as many hotels and cities, sound checks and catered meals as one sixteen-year-old would care to see. All I've ever wanted is one place to call home. Stupid, I know, but a little slice of *Seventh Heaven*, with Mr. and Mrs. Camden as my folks, the picket fence, and the freakin' dog. That's all I'm asking.

Plus, new songs mean new videos. Some kids last year talked about Crossfire's videos, like the one for "Between the Sheets," where Dad looks like a semidork, dressed in leather pants that someone else obviously picked out for him. He looked so lame, but for some reason, it hurts more when you hear someone else saying it. "I mean, please, he's thirty-nine, not twenty," some insensitive imbecile said straight to my face.

I go up to my room and close the door. All right, so fine. A new album with a new sound. Would I be a total jerk to wish they'd just call it quits this time around? When do we put rock 'n' roll past us and become a normal family, hmm? Does anybody care what I want?

I sit at my desk and stare at my favorite shot of me and my folks. I'm between them, arms around their shoulders, and my long, wavy hair is draped over their heads, like a blond three-headed monster. *Sigh*. That answers the "normal family" question.

I should check on Brianna. She was pretty pissed that I wanted to leave LA. I start a new e-mail:

From: saharagobi@crossfire.com

To: "Brianna Roman"

Subject: French Literature 101

Hey mama-san, what's up? just checking up on ya. How's LALA Land? u gotta come visit me! we got a place in coconut grove on the water, short drive from south beach. It's hot as hell here . . . 95 degrees in the shade. school's all right so far. one down, 179 to go. still incognito. I'll fill ya in later. write me back, k?

Love ya,

Desert :-)~

P.S. faith adams says hi.

Chapter Three

Desert McGraw
Smigla, Per 1
H. English

Toss a stone
Into the lake
Ripples echo

Storm clouds roll
Toward the shore
Consumed by gray

I stand alone
I don't hear
I don't see

Wash over me

I $scan$ $over$ my English homework before class starts. If Ms. Smigla doesn't like it, well too bad.

As I'm on the way back to my desk, Liam passes me and turns in his homework poem. He flashes his bright blue eyes, and something in my gut flips over. With many a desk between us, he looked like your typical, everyday guy. But now, when we squeeze in and out of the same aisle, his chest looms a lot higher than mine, and he seems, well . . . *yeah, baby!*

Let me just say for the record that I have no boyfriend and plan on keeping it that way, thanks. I have absolutely no desire to cater to a grown baby's needs this early on in my life. Brianna's boyfriend, Gus, requires twenty-four-hour roadside assistance and takes pride in the fact that his girlfriend gives him everything he needs. Well, almost everything. And it's only because of that almost-everything that she receives anything in their relationship. By dangling the little *s*-word in front of his face like a carrot in front of Bugs Bunny.

"Have you and Liam met yet?" Becca asks as I walk past her and slump into my seat.

The first few days of school I tried avoiding her, but it didn't work. We ended up talking every day in class, and now it's a whole week and a half later. The problem is, how can I tell her about myself when there's an ode to my dad written on her notebook?

"We haven't met with actual words," I say, "but that little exchange was worth a thousand of them."

"He wants to meet you, but I think he's shy."

"Shy? He doesn't seem shy."

"He can be. If he thinks a girl won't like him."

"Does he think that about me?"

"Well, you do give creepy looks sometimes. I wouldn't doubt it if that's how he sees it."

"But I— Creepy looks? Do I really?" Suddenly I'm aware of the creases on my forehead, the ones my mom loves to point out.

"That's okay. You're stressed from the move. I know," Becca says, remembering my excuse on the first day.

Right. Stressed from the move. From wondering how long I can keep up this charade, maybe, but not from the move. "Hey, Becca, if you and Liam are such good friends, how come you guys aren't hooked up?"

With her dark brown hair hanging in her face as she hustles to finish her homework, it's hard to see her expression, but I think she's hiding it on purpose. After a snifflike laugh, she says, "It's not like that between us."

Inquiring minds want to know why. I would press the issue, but she obviously doesn't want to talk about it.

The bell is about to ring, and a dozen other students hurry to complete the assignment. Am I the only one who actually does homework at home?

"Liam!" Becca calls out suddenly.

"Oh, crap! Please warn me before embarrassing me like this," I mumble, pushing back loose strands of hair, tugging at my hoop earring.

Liam comes over and crouches between us. Most of the guys

at my other school would've stood there, staring down with a hint of arrogance. But this guy is now at just the right level to hypnotize us with those piercing eyes. *My God, stop staring at him, Desert. Look away, for decency's sake.*

"Yo," Liam says.

"Yo?" Becca rests her arm around his shoulders.

Liam laughs, and I see his smile up close for the first time. It suits him. Sometimes you see a guy, think he's hot, then when he smiles, it's like, "never mind." But this . . . this is quite the specimen.

"Li, Desert. Desert, Li. She just moved here from LA," Becca informs him.

"Okay, let's leave the details of my life out of this, missy," I hear myself say, turning my attention to Liam. "Hi. Nice to meet you."

You have gorgeous, gorgeous eyes, my love. Whoops, did I just say that? Hope not.

"From LA, huh?" He tilts his head in interest.

The bell rings, and students shuffle back to their seats.

"We'll talk later." Becca shoos Liam away from her desk.

Twenty minutes into a lecture about imagery, Ms. Smigla asks us to find a buddy for an exercise. Becca's leg kicks out toward me. "Wanna work together?"

"Sure," I say. Like I have a choice.

I then notice Liam turned around, trying to send Becca some sort of telepathic message. Becca lifts up her palm, like saying, "What?" then shrugs and looks at me uncomfortably. "Um . . . do you mind working with Liam instead?"

"No, not really." So much for being shy.

Liam comes over and switches seats with Becca, who takes off to pair up with Kuntz. "Hi again," he says. "Okay if I sit with you? If not, I'll be on my way."

"No, it's cool," I answer, looking at his fine form. Yes, indeedy. I like him much better here than there.

Ms. Smig writes MESSAGE in all caps on the whiteboard then turns to face the class. "Message," she says dramatically, like she missed out on Broadway and is now trying to make up for it.

Liam and I exchange a quick glance and try not to laugh.

"A message is what you want to convey through imagery. Take a minute to come up with a few words powerful enough to create a clear message. It can be about yourself, someone else, a place, anything, but don't reveal what it's about."

Blah, blah. I check out Liam's arm. Strong. Tanned.

"For example," Ms. Smigla continues, "*fragile, porous, alive, colorful*—all adjectives to describe a coral reef, but feel free to use any part of speech you like."

Nails. Clean. Groomed.

"When you finish, trade with your partners and see if they can guess what you're describing. Go ahead."

Liam and I take deep breaths and get to work. What the heck do I write about? All I can think of is him sitting next to me. I can't write about him. What do you know about, Desert? Think. I start scribbling verbs.

reaching
begging

What else, what else. These girls in the audience, they're always . . .

pleading
crying
trying to connect

There, that's good for now. I glance over at Liam posed like Rodin's *The Thinker*, desperately trying to get his thoughts down. He sits back and surveys, lunges forward, scratches out, and rewrites. Then he looks at me, and I see that shyness Becca was talking about.

"Done?" I ask.

"Yep."

"Okay, let's switch."

He scans my paper. "Awesome," he says, like my imagery is the best he's ever read. "Is this about someone who needs help?"

"Actually, no. It's a crowd at a concert. You know, up at the stage, trying to touch a rock star like he's a god or something."

"Oh." He sighs, eyes still on the page. "Yeah, I see it. That makes sense now."

I glance at Liam's paper. His handwriting is nice and neat. I tell you, he is racking up the brownie points faster than you can say "gaga."

He's written

golden-haired, beautiful, interesting, honey-eyed

What on Earth? "Honey-eyed?" I ask. Okay, so his adjectives need a little work.

"Yeah." He shifts in his seat and nibbles on his thumbnail.

Oh, wait. This isn't about his mom. Or his dog.

He looks me square in the face. "Your eyes. They're honey brown. Very pretty," he says softly.

Now, there comes a point in a girl's life when she must differentiate between a guy's rap for the sake of pure conquest and his honest-to-God sincerity. And I'll be damned if Liam is faking this just to get a date.

"Um . . . thanks. Yours are even better." What? *Nice comeback, Des.*

"That's all right. You don't have to reciprocate."

Reciprocate? Great word! "I'm not reciprocating!"

He pretends to be taken aback by my answer, palm at his chest.

"I mean, I am, but not because you wrote that, but because it's true. Your eyes are the first thing I noticed about you."

Get a grip, Desert!

We sit there, staring at each other for a few seconds—something Marie says you should never, ever do. Brush off the compliment, keep up a casual conversation, anything, but don't stare at each other. He'll think you're desperate. Funny, but with Liam I don't feel that way.

Ms. Smigla yaps some more about the openness of imagery and what a powerful tool it can be. Ms. Smigla has never yapped truer words. And Ms. Smigla never seems to stop yapping.

Liam takes his paper and adds something else to his list. He pushes it back at me, and I read

See you at lunch, Desert?

There's a goofy face next to my name. Thank God he spelled it right. Last year Dylan, this guy I went out with, wrote *Dessert*, and I was like, holy freakin' idiot, Batman! It just ruined everything.

"I have first lunch," I whisper.

"I know," he mouths. His hand covers a smile as he waits for my reply.

From across the room I spot Becca watching us. She smiles a sad sort of smile. What's that all about? Before I could consider the implications of this little hookup, my pen writes

sure. save me a seat.

Chapter Four

Funny, Dad and the guys love to say how being in a rock 'n' roll band gives them a license to act immature and weird. So what, then, is the excuse for some of these kids in the cafeteria?

One guy is wearing a polo shirt with the collar up. He's sitting with his other *Animal House* buddies and a chick with long stringy braids, no makeup, and a headband. A headband, hear me? Then there's the perky Blondies over there, all fresh and *ohmigod!* And in this corner, weighing in at weirdness maximus, is a group of people I've come to lovingly refer to as Oyes, due to the word so liberally sprinkled throughout their Spanglish. Each of them is wearing some sort of Tommy Hilfigeresque couture. Very flattering, I must admit.

All right, all right. *Be nice, Des. Give them a chance.* Besides,

I'm sure I seem weird to them, considering I'm sitting here alone, waiting for my blue-eyed poet to appear. But it's okay. For once I don't feel like I'm in a fishbowl with everyone peering in to my life. Dare I say I feel almost normal? Mmm, this baked macaroni and cheese sure is a delicacy.

"Desert," a voice whispers by my shoulder.

I look up and see Liam standing there with his tray.

"Oh, hi!" I say, like I totally wasn't expecting him.

"I guess you were the one to save me a seat, huh?"

"This ol' space? Nah. I'm holding this for any one of my other numerous friends."

He laughs and settles down. "Sorry I'm late. I left my CD case in third period. Had to go back and get it."

"Ah. It's okay."

"Have you seen Becca?" He glances around the noisy and, might I add, smelly room.

"I just saw her in Ms. Gallo's class. Said she was skipping lunch today. That can't be healthy."

"Typical," he grumbles, popping open the plastic wrapper to his spork. "She goes off somewhere to play that guitar for a while."

I know how that goes. How many times have I seen J. C. sitting in a hotel hallway moping with his guitar? Too many to count. He always smiles up at me and says, "Hey, Des! See you tonight, baby." We never exchange too many words, but I always know he loves me like I'm his own kid, since he almost never gets to see his. The whole band treats me that way. They're like anybody's uncles, except with tattoos and nipple rings.

"Have you heard her play? Is she any good?" I ask. We could use a female teenage roadie, if only to keep me company.

Liam shrugs. "She's all right, I guess. It's kinda hard to tell with that crappy guitar. She refuses to buy a newer one."

"Why?"

"I dunno. I guess because it was her mom's. She died when Becca was real little—like five or something, in a car accident. Her dad didn't want to 'burden' Becca with memories of a mom she'd never know, so he trashed most of her stuff but let her keep the guitar."

"Geez, what an asshole."

"Yep. Then he left her here with her grandmother and went off to start a new and improved family somewhere in Chicago. So as you can imagine, Becca thinks real highly of him."

"Yeah, I can see how much he didn't want to *burden* her." I guess this would explain the sadness I've seen in Becca's eyes, even when she's smiling.

Liam digs into his mac and cheese. "At least her grandma cares about her. I feel bad for Becca sometimes, but that's how she deals with stuff, going off somewhere to be alone."

Hmm, sad. Okay, now ask him something, Desert, before he starts asking about you.

"So how come you moved to Miami?" Liam inquires.

Damn, cut off at the pass. "No big deal," I lie. "My dad is working here now."

"Mmm-hmm," he mutters, nodding his head like a psychotherapist. "And, let me guess, you're resenting him for having

27

ripped you out of your normal routine in LA?"

Ha! Good one! "No, not quite. I'm actually very happy to be here."

"You sound like a game show contestant."

"Thank you, Mr. . . . "

"Blanco."

"Mr. Blanco, could I please say hi to my mom who's in the audience?"

"Why yes, of course!"

"Hi, Mom!" I wave to an invisible crowd. "Thank you, I'll take Birds of Prey for five hundred dollars please, Mr. Blanco."

Liam lets out a hearty laugh. "Silly," he mumbles, shaking his head.

Cutie. And a Hispanic cutie at that. Bonus, *mi amor*. He's a bowl full of cherries. Brianna would hate him.

"By the way," he says. "I hope you don't think I'm weird because of what I wrote in Smig's class."

"Weird? You?" I ask, looking over the Oyes, Blondies, and Animal Housers. "Never."

"You probably think I'm some stalker now."

"Well, you did know which lunch I was in."

"I guess I've just noticed you, that's all. Hey, speaking of stalkers, which way do you go home?"

"Very funny," I say, shooting him a half-serious look. "Sometimes my mom picks me up. Sometimes I like to walk."

"You what?" He looks like a rat that's been dropped in a snake pit. "You don't walk in Miami unless you really have to!"

"What makes you think I don't have to?" Paranoia alert! Does he know something he's not telling me?

"You just said sometimes your mom picks you up and sometimes you like to walk. Nobody here *likes* walking home."

"I do." My tour bus, globe-trotting mentality is showing its true colors. After being cooped up for hours of traveling, the band's entourage, me included, likes to walk in the cities we visit. It keeps us from going insane.

"Do you want us to give you a ride home?" Liam asks.

"Us? Who's us?"

"Me and my brother, Michael. He's a senior. I can ask him if he'll drive you home so you don't have to walk. He won't mind."

Nothing would make this new life seem more normal than being driven home by a sweet guy like Liam Blanco, but no. Not a good idea.

"Liam, it's okay, really. I don't live far from here. It's just a few blocks. I'll be fine."

"You sure?"

"Yeah, I'm sure." *I'm sure I don't want you to see the castle I live in and wonder why I don't have a stretch limo picking me up.*

"Well, if you ever get tired of walking, let me know."

"Thanks." I smile.

The lunch bell rings. I need more time with him. We've kidded around a bunch today, but I still don't know a whole lot about him.

Like he's heard my thoughts, he rips a sheet of paper out of a notebook and scribbles his phone number. "Here," he says, folding and handing it to me, "in case you get bored this weekend."

I stand there like a dork, feeling like Baby telling Johnny, "I carried a watermelon" in the movie *Dirty Dancing*. Okay, I know, I know . . . I *must* stop watching old flicks on AMC.

But I, unlike Baby, am suave. I don't let too much time go by without a witty response. I am in control of this situation. I am—

"Okay, I'll call you."

—Such a loser.

After school I zip out fast, in case Liam decides to check up on me. I'm about half a block down Main Avenue when I hear Becca's voice calling me from behind. "Desert!"

Oh, joy.

"Hey!" I turn around with mock surprise. "What's up?"

"Where are you headed? Millionaires' Row?" She cracks up at the idea.

I laugh a little nervously. "Yeah, right! Nah, I was gonna stop at the 7-Eleven."

Now shoo, go home.

"Listen, last week, you said you liked my gig bag, and I mean . . . I don't know of anyone who knows what that's called. Most people say 'guitar case.'"

Oops.

"Do you play guitar?" she asks with hope in her voice.

"Um . . . no, I don't, actually. I just heard a friend say 'gig bag' once. He has a . . . garage band back in LA." *Yes, nice recovery!*

"Really? That's so great. I don't think I could ever be in a band.

I think I'd be more of a solo artist. So you at least like guitar, then?"

"Well, yeah." *I guess you could say I've been forced into liking it.*

"Would you mind if I came over to your house sometime? I could play some songs for you, see what you think of them."

"Umm." My brilliant responses have a way with me. "My house is still a horrendous mess of boxes. Why don't I go to yours instead?"

"Wherever. I just meant get together. Are you doing anything this weekend?" She squints at me in the afternoon sun.

I want to tell her, "Actually, your favorite band has their first recording session at South Beach Sounds this weekend, and I'd really like to hear the wonderful new implementation of Faith Adams's amazing input. 'Dance tonight, dance tonight, rock your body, feel all right.' Yeah!"

But instead . . . "I can't this weekend, Becca. I promised my folks I'd get my room organized. Next Saturday, maybe? We can order pizza or something."

Becca looks down at her sneakers and then seems to compare mental notes of her wardrobe versus mine. "Okay," she answers finally, a little disappointed. "We'll talk on Monday . . . or call me if you want. You have my number."

"All right." I try to smile real friendly. "Later!"

She flashes me a peace sign. I watch her head off into the *other* part of the Grove, the not-so-nice part. I feel really bad about not hanging with her, but I've just *got* to witness the musical merger of classic rock and teen pop. C.R.O.P., they should call it. It sounds a lot like *crap*.

I'm heading into my neighborhood, a lively mélange of oaks and palms lining the street. Bougainvillea and hibiscus blossoms litter the sidewalk like confetti. This is the part of Miami they show in postcards—except in postcards you can't smell this bittersweet bite of salty air. Should I call Liam tonight after the session? No, we get out too late. That's all right, I shouldn't call so soon anyway. I'll e-mail Brianna instead.

Our house is easily the prettiest one at the end of the cul-de-sac, with the backyard facing Biscayne Bay. Dad's outside, in shorts and a baseball cap, picking up the paper. It's two-thirty in the afternoon. Why can't he pick up the morning paper in the morning, like any normal human being? I'm trotting up the garden path toward him when I hear the low, rumbling sound of an engine not too far behind me. I turn around and spot a car facing our house that wasn't there a minute ago. A stalker, for sure.

Just as I'm flipping a graceful bird at whoever it may be, a great big zoom lens appears out of the passenger window and someone snaps a picture.

Chapter Five

At South Beach Sounds, later that night, things suck.

"I don't believe this." Mom speaks to no one in particular, a wisp of smoke curling from her mouth. She only smokes when she's aggravated. Like now.

From the couch Marie and I keep our lips zipped. We know better than to speak when she's like this.

"Did you see who else was with him, Desert?" she snaps again, just as I'm noticing she's got the same creases on her forehead as I did when Becca deemed me creepy looking.

"No, Mom. Sorry. Couldn't even tell you for sure it was a guy. All we saw was a camera, so we went inside, and that was it."

"Jesus!" She flails her arms then paces to the glass that separates us from Dad, Faith, J. C., and Ryan in the sound booth.

Max and Phil are off somewhere working on rhythm. She exhales her smoke and leans her forehead against the cool panel. "That was a tabloid shot, Marie. How did that happen so quickly?"

Marie gets up from the couch and stretches, her arms in the air. "I wish I knew, Matti. You want me to look into it?"

"That would be *ideal*, thank you," Mom says, her reflection in the glass showing major annoyance.

Marie looks at me and makes an ugly face. I make an ugly face back. If only Mom knew how much we made fun of her when she's not looking. Marie then flips open her cell phone and starts investigating while pouring herself some coffee.

I look at my mom over there. She looks tired. I know what she's thinking: Why can't people just leave us the hell alone already?

Over the years lots of journalists have written about Matti Thomas McGraw being one of the only women in the music business to raise her child on the road, pointing out how the rock 'n' roll lifestyle can't be too good for a toddler. And it's kind of true, for the most part. Most other wives stay home and take care of the kids, while the musician dads revel in the fantasy world of the music business.

I know it must be hard for her to take all that stress, but you know what? It doesn't have to be this way. She could hire someone else to take her place. We could stay home, flip pancakes together. But we've beaten this topic into the ground. She's already said it—"I'd rather jump off the Brooklyn Bridge than be told how I should live my life."

So it's pretty much a lost cause. The only chance of me having one place to call home is if Crossfire stops touring, and now that seems highly unlikely. Besides, touring is how we've always paid the bills, says my mom. Crossfire puts on the best live shows out there.

In the sound booth, however, is a ray of hope. The Faith-Flesh liaison is getting off to a rocky start. Looks like it's not coming together. Dad keeps glancing over at Mom with a frustrated look, but he never loses his cool. It's always amazing to me how my dad's stage act is so different from his real self. Everyone thinks he's this wild, emotional dude, throwing himself on his knees while reaching out to the crowd, when really he's calm and hard-working. I totally believe that it's him who's kept this whole enterprise together for so many years.

I see him shaking his head, taking a pen from behind his ear, writing, putting the pen back, crooning, and shaking his head again. It could easily take forever to hear them work on one, complete song.

"Mom?" I ask. "Can I please go for a walk?"

She pulls away from the glass and settles down at her laptop, concentrating on her keyboard. "Not right now, hon." *Tappy-tappy-tap.*

"Why?"

"Desert, honey, if the press already knows where we live, I don't want you going out there right now. This is the next place they'll come looking for shots of us. You want to be in tomorrow's papers? Go right ahead."

Great. That's the last thing I need is for everyone at school to know who I am so soon. You see why my life sucks? Liam and Becca don't ever have to deal with this controlling crap. Then I stop to think about Becca. I can't believe what Liam said about her dad. And her dead mom's guitar. God, that's so sad. Maybe I *will* go over her house this weekend and listen to her play.

Max and Phil come in, sniffing for sushi. "Desi!" Max cries, touching the top of my head like I'm still three years old. "The girls are visiting in a few months, so you'll have someone to share this boredom with."

"Janie and Jocelyn. Coming to join the fun," I say.

Max's nine-year-old twins are so lucky. They live in Arizona with their mom, Linda. They don't tag along. Neither do Phil's kids. See? It really pisses me off.

"Yep," Max says with a smile, like he can't wait. "They'll be on Christmas break." He points to the sushi. "You hogging dinner all for yourself?"

"No," I say, punching his leg. "But leave me some, you slobbish pig."

He laughs. This is normal between us. I love Maxie-Max.

But then Max sees Dad's death-look through the sound booth window, drops the wasabi back in its place, and picks up his drumsticks. Silent Phil follows suit, grabbing his bass from the corner where he set it down, and they go back out into the hall. My dad has succeeded in transmitting telepathically, "When we're all finished, we *all* eat."

My stomach is grumbling, and even though I know he wouldn't mind if *I* ate, I decide to wait. I pull a scrap of paper from my back pocket. Liam's phone number. He's such a nice guy. This would be too weird for him if he found out. Maybe I was better off at St. Alf's, where at least I wasn't the only kid with famous parents. I won't call him tonight. Maybe tomorrow.

Mom gets up to stand in the doorway to the sound engineer's room, so I take over her laptop to kill some time. I switch user profiles from hers to mine and log in. Let's see if Brianna has anything interesting to report. It's strange that I haven't spoken to her in weeks. That's the longest we've ever gone without talking.

Open new e-mail:

From: saharagobi@crossfire.com
To: "Brianna Roman"
Subject: Geometry

hello? anybody home? earth to Bri, come in Bri. i met this guy who's way cooler than Gus, jk. how is Gus anyway? still grabbing your butt in public? so, his name's Liam Blanco, as in William White. lol!! what's going on at st. alf? have you seen Dylan? does he carry around the dictionary I gave him for his birthday? I'm actually liking my school. did you know the crappy cars here don't only belong to the teachers? miss you, mama-san. come in, Bri.

Love ya,

Desert :-D

PS faith adams wants your autograph

I log off. Marie's next to me, sipping her coffee and trying to get a good signal, but her cell phone keeps failing her. I wonder if she's heard from Brianna. "Babalú, do you know anything about Bri? She's like, lost."

"No," she says, pushing buttons, then giving up and shoving the thing into her pocket. "Haven't talked to my niece in a while."

"Whatever. She's probably busy with school. So what's with Faith?" I ask, eyeing the sushi just sitting there, begging us all to come, eat, and be merry.

"Nothing." She sighs. "Hopefully she'll inject some youth angst into the songs, something the last set was missing."

"But why? I mean, they're not teenagers," I say, looking at my dad and the guys. "It wouldn't make sense for them to write about our problems."

"Maybe not, but listeners want something universal that everyone can relate to."

"But that's pop! I mean, *hello*?" Is this not obvious?

Marie shrugs. "Whatever it's called, that's what Crossfire needs."

That's what Crossfire needs? I don't want to tell Mom how to do her job or anything, but isn't that what Marie is for, to advise against dumb decisions? Whatever.

"Where is she staying?" As far away from us as possible, hopefully.

"Right now, downtown, until your dad sets her up in your spare room."

"What? My house? Oh, puh-leez!" I cross my arms. This happens a lot, people who collaborate with us temporarily get invited to stay at the McGraws'—by none other than Flesh himself. But Faith is dangerous! And not to mention ugly!

My mother turns around in the doorway. "It's just while they're working on lyrics. Maybe two months or so."

"Two months with Faith? I don't believe this. You better get a force field around your bedroom door. She's after Dad."

"Desert, your father's not like that," she says, turning back to the soundproof glass, "so please relax."

Why? Why must I always relax? I'm relaxed just fine, thank you! Okay. Think positive. Think happy thoughts. Think . . . Liam.

I turn to Marie and whisper, "I met a guy."

"Oh, yeah?" she says with a hint of protective tigress in her voice. "After only two weeks in town? What's he like?"

On the other side of the glass, Dad gets up and starts pacing. This is not good.

"He's nice. Not a jerk, real cute. I think he likes me. Well, hopefully. We'll see."

Marie nods, agreeing. If Marie approves of the guy, that's usually a good sign. She didn't like Dylan.

Sigh. Boring! Let me outta here. I want to walk Ocean Drive, but Mom's right. The same studio used by dozens of other famous bands is exactly where more photographers are likely to be waiting.

On some nights the creative juices overflow, and we can feel the electricity in our bones. The separate parts—drums, guitar, bass, and vocals—all click together like magic, and poof, you've got a musical work of art. But some nights leave us wondering how on earth we're gonna repay our hardworking fans who shell out the bucks for Crossfire CDs, live shows, and concert DVDs.

At 11:00 P.M. Faith Adams looks frazzled. Poor baby. She piles a napkin with sushi and shovels the pieces into her mouth. No one speaks much except for Marie, who's back on her cell phone yelling at God knows who. Max and Phil snort and swallow their food. Dad's not hungry, I guess. He opts for a diet Coke with lemon, then pens twenty minutes' worth of lyrics before chucking them all into the trash.

I wonder how much I could get for those on eBay.

Chapter Six

Holy cow. Becca lives here? Looks like the butt end of a bigger house. It's an efficiency, underneath a bunch of banana and umbrella trees, bougainvillea, and palms that look nothing like the ones on Rodeo Drive. The screened door squeaks when Becca opens it.

"Hey! You found it okay?"

You mean, did I machete my way through dense jungle foliage only to locate an inhabited shed? "Yeah, it was no problem. Nice place," I say, impressing myself with my straight face.

Becca lifts an eyebrow at me. "This is a no-sarcasm zone, Desert. Didn't you see the sign when you came through the gate?"

"I'm serious. It's very . . . uh . . . secluded, tropical. Lots of people would love to live here." *Offhand, I can't think of anyone.*

"I thought you couldn't come over this weekend," she says, letting me in.

"Oh, I finished my room, so I thought, 'Why not?'" Actually, there was another session at the studio this morning, and if I had to endure any more torture, I would've ruined the recording with the sound of my head banging on a wall.

"Did you eat? Wanna order that pizza?"

"Sure, why not."

Becca hits the programmed number for Papa John's on her corded (read: ancient) phone and orders a two-large special with cheesesticks. Yum! Now I'm starting to like this little hut. Even if the A/C unit in the window groans while spewing only slightly chilled air. At least she has terrazzo floors!

"Where's your grandma?" I ask.

"Next door. Hanging out at Didi's."

"Who?"

"Her best friend. Saturdays are flowerpot-painting days."

"Ah. No brothers or sisters?"

"Yeah, I have a sister. She's twenty-one, works in Gainesville. I saw your mom dropping you off. Nice car," she says casually.

Mom drives an Accord, which is quite a surprise if you think about it. I guess that says something about her response to fame. Anyone can drive a Porsche once they have the cash. It takes someone zany enough, someone who names her children after landforms, to drive a car so far below her means. Me, I would've taken the Acura NSX.

"Thanks. She's promised it to me for my birthday." Actually, she promised me anything under forty thousand, but no need to mince words.

"Lucky you." Becca sighs. "I'll be happy if I get a scooter."

Becca's room is the size of my closet, but I like it. Pictures of guitarists cover the walls. Jimi Hendrix. Eddie Van Halen. Eric Clapton. The Edge. And J. C., but I try not to notice that one. The twin-size bed is against the wall. Her guitar is uncovered, on its side in front of sheet music.

Oh, would you look at that. The music is for "Between the Sheets." Dad would be honored. I, on the other hand, am mortified. If Becca and I are going to stay friends, I've got to tell her about my family somehow, when the time is right. But this isn't it.

"Cool room. It says a lot about you."

"You think so?" she asks, glancing around. "I guess it says some things."

"It reflects your interests, anyway." I drop my purse next to the closet and myself in front of her stereo. She sits on the floor, back against her bed.

"What kind of music do you listen to?" she asks.

Ah, the million-dollar question. "Well, I'm pretty eclectic. My collection's got everything—rock, classical, rap, reggae, emo." Yes, emo.

"Do you listen to bands like The Madmen?"

"Ha! You actually call them a band? Shouldn't playing your own instruments be a requirement before calling yourself a band?

The Madmen owe their existence to Faith Adams's theatrics and that's about it."

Becca stares at me wide-eyed, like she doesn't know what to think of that.

"I know, I know," I say, remembering a boy "band" I saw on TRL complaining about what makes a band a band. "A band is any group of people who make music together, even if they're only humming. Go ahead, let the backlash begin."

"No, you're right," she says. "That's exactly how I feel."

Well, alrighty! "See? I knew I liked you for a reason."

Becca smiles that melancholy smile again. "Faith is cool and everything, but if you strip her of all that glam, there's not much substance there."

"Exactly!" Exactly.

Becca's eyes light up. "I think creating meaningful lyrics has got to be one of the hardest parts of writing songs. To come up with words, like Smig was saying, powerful enough to convey a message. I totally respect anyone who can put their thoughts down like that. I can't do it."

"Oh, I'm sure you can. You're in Honors English!" I laugh.

She's not laughing. "Seriously. I can't. Every time I try it, the words come out sounding like slop, with not even the slightest fraction of the emotion I was feeling when writing them."

"Maybe it takes practice."

"Maybe it takes talent."

I smile. "Talent's overrated. Lots of people with talent get nowhere without practice."

"That's true. Look, read these," she urges, pushing the CD insert for *Crossfire—Insanity* into my hands. "This is what I'm talking about."

Oh, goody.

Becca flips to a song called "Wilderness," a song I happen to know very well because my dad wrote it next to me on a bus ride to the Meadowlands. He wrote it after having a huge fight with my mom that morning.

"'Darkness spreads its wings over my bitter heart,'" she recites, gazing somewhere over the rainbow. "Isn't that beautiful?"

"I guess. It's kinda corny."

"Corny? Desert, can't you hear the pain this man was feeling when he wrote that? That anguish of being distant from someone you love? To put that raw emotion out there for everyone to hear? It's amazing anyone could do that."

"Mmm-hmm." Damn, she's pretty good. I don't remember her being on that bus ride.

"You don't seem to think so."

"No, I do! I agree. What else you got?" *Get me out of here, this is scaring me.*

"There's lots more, but Flesh writes the best lyrics of any songwriter by far." She reaches behind her and pulls back the closet door, revealing an early poster of my dad in his wild child days, long hair, no shirt, a hand down his pants. "Isn't he awesome?"

If someone could just get me a bucket, I'd like to barf now. "He's probably not what he seems," I tell her.

"What do you mean? He's well known for being totally sincere and openhearted with everything, from his songs down to his interviews."

"Yeah, I know, but still, famous people are always different once you get to know them. So I've heard."

"I guess that could be true. He's probably got ten cats and loves bubble baths, right?"

Let's not go crazy. "Who knows? Maybe."

Becca picks up her guitar and strums a few chords. My stomach growls. I hope she didn't hear that. She starts into something that sounds like it could be Indigo Girls, but it's not. It's totally Becca. And it's good. Really good. She must, and I mean *must*, get better strings. Maybe I can sneak her some. But the whole vibe is there. I listen and the more I do, the more I feel something stronger coming through.

Becca goes out on her own. There's no me, no CDs scattered about, no cat on the floor next to her. There are no walls around her. Just music rising out of her guitar, at the expense of what seems to be a very broken heart. She lets the last note trail off like a kiss in the wind and drops her head onto the curve of the instrument. That's when her sobbing begins.

Okay. Maybe I shouldn't be here. She's forgotten she's not alone. I'll just be going now. *No, wait, Des!* Whatever the matter is, this girl has just let me into her soul. Through music. *Stay.*

Becca looks up, wiping her tearstained face. "I'm sorry."

"Don't be. That was great!"

"Don't lie. I'm just a moron who'll never learn to play right."

Excuse me? "Um . . . Becca, I beg to differ. You play better than some people who've been taking lessons for years. Why are you crying? You okay?"

"Desert," she begins, "you know how you asked why Liam and I haven't hooked up?"

"Yeah?" Oh, Christ, she *does* have a thing for Liam! I knew it!

"And I've told you how that wouldn't happen?"

"Yeah? Becca, I think he's really cute and all, but if you want him, you need to tell—"

"I'm gay, Desert."

Oh.

"You can freak out now if I've scared you," she says.

And I thought *my* secret was big.

"What? Why would that scare me? I didn't know that, but it doesn't scare me." Actually, it scares me a little.

"Of course you didn't know. It's not like I have a sign on my forehead."

"All right, you're the one who said this was a no-sarcasm zone, not me. Look, I'm fine with that, really. I mean, I'm not gay, but that doesn't mean we can't be friends, right?"

She wipes her eyes with the inside of her shirt. "That's what kills me. Anyone I ever meet that I'm remotely interested in is never interested in me."

Is she talking about me? 'Cause that would really make me feel crappy. "I'm interested in you. I don't have to be gay to be interested in you as a person, do I?"

She smiles sadly. "Thanks, but you know what I mean."

"I know." I don't really, but what else can I say?

47

"I'll never find someone. It's so hard."

"Of course you'll find someone, Becca. You're a very pretty girl with a beautiful soul. You just showed me."

We sit quietly for a minute.

"Nobody knows, except Liam, so please don't go broadcasting it."

"No problem."

Becca exhales deeply. "I don't mean anything by telling you this, okay? I don't expect anything from you. Just wanted you to know, that's all."

"Okay. I appreciate it."

Now what?

For the next few minutes, we don't speak. Becca tunes the guitar and continues to space out like I'm not there. We need something to get this ball rolling again.

"Pizza!" the delivery boy shouts, knocking so loud on the front door that even the cat meows out of a deep sleep.

Thank the sweet Lord. Food.

Chapter Seven

Shadows enfold, shadows embrace
Through a dark veil, behind the face
Hides a deep void, a sleeping cocoon
Butterfly waits, freedom come soon
Will you accept me? Will you believe?
Will you cast stones at what you perceive?
I need you to love me, a sleeping cocoon
Unfolding my wings, freedom come soon

Late in the afternoon Mom enters the kitchen, interrupting my poetry session. The look on her face spells you-better-have-a-good-explanation. "Desert, someone's here to see you."

"What? I haven't told anyone where we live! Don't look at me like that, Mother!" I jump off the island stool and head toward the foyer.

What the hell?

"Becca! How did you—?"

"Find out you live here?" Her expression is one of hurt and shock. "You took out papers from your bag to make room for the CDs I lent you, then left them on the floor. Your schedule," she says, holding it up, eyebrows raised, like any idiot could recognize the neighborhood, "has your address on it."

Oh.

Blood drains from my face. She goes on. "Millionaires' Row. Thanks for telling me." She hands me the schedule by the very corner like it has cooties. I guess she could've sliced my face with it if she wanted to.

"So I live here, what's the big deal?" I mean, really.

"Nothing, except you were basically laughing at my house the whole time you were there."

That is so dumb. "No, I wasn't."

"If I had known this, I wouldn't have invited you over. No wonder you didn't want me coming here."

"I really did have to organize my room."

"You lied to me."

"I haven't lied to you about anything!"

"Well, you sure as hell didn't tell me you were rich!"

I think that's the first time I ever heard someone call me that. It almost sounds like an insult.

"All right, so what was I supposed to say to you? Hi, Becca, I'm Desert, and my parents have lots of money? Is that what I should've said? I don't care about that, so why should you?"

"Well, not telling something is the same as lying. You're withholding information."

"Girls?" My mother has joined us in the foyer. "Would you like to come in and argue somewhere a little more comfortable?" Her polite way of scolding me for acting like a dumb-ass.

Becca and I look at each other, a little embarrassed. "Sorry," I tell her. "I should've said something. Wanna come in? This is my mom, Matti."

Becca smiles nervously. "Hi." She then takes her first real look around. Her eyes soar up to the ceiling at the entrance chandelier. The marble staircase. The parquet floors. She's in awe. "Nice shack."

I laugh, showing her in. "Come in, dork. Sorry about the mess."

Mom's been unpacking some of the boxes today, so there's kitchen stuff all over the counters. And the dining room, and practically everywhere. Dad's been—wait a second! "Mom? Where's Dad?"

She must pick up the panic in my voice, since she says, "Hmm, probably in his cave," and runs off to make sure he doesn't come out of his private studio for anything while Becca's here.

"Didn't you say your father was an artist?" Becca asks, picking up a slotted spoon, running her fingers along it like it's made of gold or something. Fine, so it's silver.

"Yeah, he is."

"But not a starving artist, I can see that." She puts down the spoon and picks up a bottle of Cristal instead.

"My mom's a manager," I say, like it's her career and not much else that explains how we live. Obviously, that doesn't work.

"A manager?" she laughs. "Of what, Microsoft?"

"Something like that." Behind her, I spot the *Billboard* and American Music awards being used as stops to the dining room door. *Must evacuate the premises, quick!* "Wanna see my room?"

"Okay, but can I check out this place first? Your house, it's so . . . beautiful. I've always dreamed of living somewhere like this."

She doesn't understand. It's not all that great. "Um . . . sure. Here, let me show you. Living room, dining room, great room, patio, pool, garage, guest bath. Now, wanna see my room?" Big smile.

"Oh, my God!" Her hands fly to her mouth, eyes like saucers.

Oh, no! She saw the family portrait, or a Crossfire poster, or my dad waving to her from outside, I just know it.

"That's your backyard?" she cries, gliding over to the French doors, opening them up. The hot breeze from the bay swoops in and surrounds us.

It's an incredible afternoon, and I can see why she's amazed. The water is glistening like diamonds in the dying sun. Dozens of sailboats line the horizon. Jet Skis and wave runners circle each other, like kids playing tag. Pelicans sit on posts, lazily watching the view.

I guess I never really noticed how nice it is out here.

Becca skips over to the pool, following its curve like a yellow brick road. I hadn't exactly thought of what to tell her about my dad, but I have to think of something quick. Mom can't keep him captive in the studio all night. Not what I had in mind for breaking the news.

"Becca, I've gotta tell you something."

She turns around to face me. "If it's about what I told you, I didn't mean to make you uncomfortable or make you think I'm after you."

"No, no, that's not what I was gonna say."

"I'm almost sorry I said anything, 'cause now you'll think I'm weird."

"I don't think you're weird. Well, maybe a little."

Her sense-of-humor meter is on low as she stares at me for a second, scanning my eyes, reading my face. Then it kicks in. She grins big and shakes her head.

"Kidding!" I say.

"Sometimes I'm not sure."

"Look, what I was gonna say is . . ."

Damn. How do I do this? I can't just tell her straight out. She'll faint. "Let's sit over there." I walk her to the patio chairs, underneath the big sun umbrella. "Becca, we're friends, right?"

"I should hope so."

"Good, 'cause you know how you had this great big secret to tell me but were afraid to? You thought I'd take it the wrong way?"

"Yeah?"

"Well, it's only fair that I let you in on something too, but you have to promise, no . . . swear, swear you won't tell anybody, okay?"

"Sure. What is it?" she asks, palm to her heart. "You're scaring me!"

"Sweetie?" Mom's back, rounding the pool and wringing her hands. "I haven't found Daddy. Have you seen him?" She lowers her stare to let me know that Flesh, lead singer of Crossfire, is running loose on the grounds somewhere and we must catch him. Quickly.

"No, I thought he was in the studio!" Crap! *Crap!* She can't see him before I tell her!

"No, honey, only Faith."

"Studio?" Becca's eyebrows shoot up.

"Yeah . . . um . . . photo studio, my dad's a photographer, I mean, no, he's not. Okay, Becca, look . . ."

Becca's head turns back and forth to examine my nervous face, then my mom's, then once again past my shoulder, to see—

Dad comes out of the pool shed, wearing his Rock Is Dead cap and brandishing the bug-net pole over his shoulder. "Hey, girly!"

No! Not like this! Aauuughhh!

"Desert!" Becca whispers, leaning into me. "That guy, he looks exactly like . . ." There's a long silence, except for the buzzing of mosquitoes and the Jet Skis out on the ocean.

And then she's done. No peep. No scream. Nothing. Just her eyes rolling back into her head as she slumps out of the patio chair.

Chapter Eight

"*I could tell you,* but then I'd have to destroy you."

"You think this is funny, Desert? Tell me what's going on!"

I think Becca already knows what's going on. She's just waiting for me to say it and make it official. "Fine, just lower your voice, will you? Geez. All right, look." I pause, thinking of an excellent beginning for my shocking revelation. "You know how everyone has a mother and a father?"

She's not amused.

Okay, here goes nothing. "Well, my father just happens to be Richard McGraw. So how've you been?" *Brace. Brace yourself.*

"What?!!"

And we're off!

"Flesh?! As in *Flesh*?! Your dad?!" A concert-worthy scream pierces the house, and somewhere in the woods, a deer and several bunnies lift their dainty heads to listen.

This is going so well. "Um . . . yep. Pretty cool, huh?"

Her face searches mine for any sign of a joke. "Yep, pretty cool?! Is that all you can say?"

Oh, no, no, I have lots more sarcasm where that came from! "Becca, I know this is freaking you out, but try to relax, okay?"

"Relax? You want me to relax? Right, okay, Desert, I'll relax!" She stands and starts pacing my bedroom frantically. "I can't believe this! This isn't happening! This isn't happening!" Trembling, she takes the glass of water Mom left her and sips, trying not to choke.

"Believe me, I understand," I try empathizing.

Her eyes, they resemble something like a raving lunatic's. "No. No, I don't think you do. This is un-*freakin'*-believable, okay?! How's my hair?" She runs a hand through her long bangs.

"Your hair's fine."

"This is Flesh's house?" She's gonna cry. Uh-oh, there we go.

I hand her a couple of tissues. "Richard McGraw's house. Try thinking of him that way. My dad. A totally normal, run-of-the-mill human being."

She stops and gapes at me like I need a vocab review on words like *normal*. "Normal? He is anything *but* normal, Desert! He is the greatest songwriter *ever*, a legend. He rules!"

All right, let's see, how can I put this? "Becca, he eats, sleeps, takes dumps like anyone else. He's normal, okay?"

Her eyes light up. "Does Liam know about this?"

"No, and you can't tell him either! If you tell him, I will definitely kill you!"

"You haven't told anyone?"

"No, ma'am." I shake my head.

She wilts into my desk chair and looks up all weary. "So you're that 'teenage daughter' they've mentioned in articles. Why didn't I notice this?"

"Honestly, I have no clue. My name's on dozens of fan websites, too. I'm surprised no one at school's recognized it yet, especially you, Miss Huge Crossfire Fan! Shouldn't you have known?"

"I don't have a computer." She scans my collection of movie posters and photos from all the cities we visited on tour last year. "Look at this room! I've never seen a bedroom so huge!"

And I wanted the bigger one down the hall. "I know you're in shock, but just try to relax."

"Stop telling me to relax, Desert! This is like Becca in Freakin' Wonderland! Do you know what a nothing life I've had? This is the biggest thing that's ever happened to me!"

Somehow I doubt that, considering her past, but I'll just keep my mouth shut.

"Here I was, mad at you because you hadn't told me where you lived, as if that wasn't enough, and then out pops Flesh, like the pool guy from the fourth dimension!"

"I know. This seems weird to you."

"Excuse me, weird *as hell* is more like it."

"Fine, but this hasn't been easy on me, either. I *was* going to tell you."

"When? When were you gonna tell me? Were you gonna invite me over for dinner and spring him on me between soup and salad?"

"There was never a good time, Becca."

She stops, looking defeated. "You know, I don't know if I should hug you or beat the crap out of you."

"Look, I was waiting until we were good friends, but that didn't happen until today."

Silence. She's satisfied. *Thank God!*

Becca takes a deep breath, trying to absorb everything. "Matti McGraw," she says slowly. "Now I recognize the name. 'Special thanks to Des.' I've read that in every CD insert."

"That would be *moi*."

She snorts at her own inability to put two and two together sooner. "Great. Now he thinks I'm a total loser for fainting in front of him." She buries her face in her hands.

"Hey, look on the bright side. At least you didn't make a fool of yourself when he carried you up the stairs!"

Becca squeals and shakes her head over and over. "I was unconscious? Oh, God, I'm such an idiot, idiot, idiot!"

"No, you're not. Look, don't worry, he's used to it."

"Where's he now?" she mumbles, glancing up.

"I don't know. Let's find out, so you can get this over with." I jump off the bed and head toward the door, but Becca starts again.

"No! No, I can't!" she whines, shaking her hands like they hurt. Her head drops into her lap. "Oh, God! This isn't happening! Do you know how many times I've dreamed of this? Now I actually meet him, and I'm totally flipping out!"

Oh, for crying out loud. "You want a shot of whiskey?"

She looks up, blinking. "What?"

"Come on, let's go find Flesh."

Becca clings painfully to my arm, all the way down the hall, down the stairs, and across the house. It's about to fall off. "Hang in there, Lion. The great and powerful Oz will see you now." Slowly I open the door to the studio.

"Oh, my God, oh, my God," Becca whimpers to herself, afraid to look inside. When she finally spots him, a screech escapes her lips, but she immediately shoves her face into my arm to mute it.

Dad's alone on the couch, an assortment of paper scraps scattered around him. Ripped notebook pages on the seat cushions, cocktail napkins on his knees, and sticky notes on his arms. He looks like the Amazing Post-It Man—more powerful than a paper cut!

He hears Becca's imitation of a cat getting skinned and, to my relief, puts on a sappy smile, the kind a giant might wear for a frightened baby. Between that, the ripped shorts, and flip-flops, he looks nothing like the poster boy Becca expects. In fact, he looks like Jimmy Buffett.

"Hi," he greets Becca, standing up. Leaves of paper fall to the floor.

"H-h-i-i!" *Ouch!* I pry her fingernails out of my arm.

His hand goes out to her gently. "I'm Desert's dad, Rich."

Good, Dad, good!

Becca stares at it for a couple of seconds, like it's a figment of her imagination. Then she takes it. "I'm Becca. Rebecca. Reese. Rebecca Reese. Nice to meet you . . . finally . . . Flesh . . . sir."

"Sir?" He laughs, holding her hand for a moment. "Same here, Becca."

Her breath quickens at hearing the almighty Flesh speak her name, and I can see her struggling to control it. Otherwise, I'd say she's doing pretty good. Dad smiles, then acts like a klutz, pretending to fall backward over the mess. I know he's doing it to make her feel at ease. He lands on the couch and sighs real big.

"So what're you doing in this mess, Dad?" Small talk for Becca's sake. I know exactly what he's doing.

"Just trying to organize my thoughts." He glances around at the work spread out around him. Lyrics. He meant lyrics but didn't want to use any lingo that would remind our guest of his alter ego.

"Hey, Dad, did you know that Becca plays guitar?" I know how much he *loves* it when I put him on the spot.

Silence, the kind that means he'll kill me later. He hates it when mediocre musicians talk to him about how they, too, are in a rock band, headed toward surefire stardom. "Really?" he answers with a smile, fake interest all over his face. At least I think it's fake.

Becca spits out a goofy laugh. "Desert! No, I don't! What're you talking about?" She starts biting her nails. I've never seen her bite her nails.

"Becca, don't be modest. You should hear her, Dad."

"I don't play! I suck. I just mess around, that's all." Nail fragments fly to the floor.

"You write your own songs?" Dad asks, way out of character. Or is he?

"No! God, no! Well, sometimes. I have some songs, I mean, that I wrote, but mostly, I just play your songs, other songs, I mean!"

"That's not true," I interrupt. "You played one today that was yours. I know it was."

Are her eyes glowing red at me? "No, I didn't! That was nothing." She turns to my dad and grins nervously. "It was nothing."

Now should I embarrass her further and ask her to play it for him? This could be so much fun!

"Any lines to go with them?" Dad inquires.

"*Nooo*, definitely not. I can't write lyrics to save my life."

She's right about that. I saw her homework poem.

Dad slouches back on the couch, sighing heavily. "Desert can. She doesn't think she can write, but she can. Ask her to show you sometime."

"Um . . . hello? Leave me out of this. Who cares, Dad?"

"I do. You're a gifted writer. You should put it to good use."

"Good use? My words get some pretty good use right where they are, in my head, in private, not all over the place for everyone and their mother to see, thank you very much."

"Is this yours?" he asks, holding up my poem, the one I was writing in the kitchen when Becca showed up.

"Yes, that's mine! Give it back, scavenger!" I can't believe him!

"It's strong, Desert. I like it."

"Yeah, well, it's not yours to read! It's for school."

As much as he's enjoying this, he gives it back without a fight. "It's what good lyrics are made of."

"I don't care." He's not going to start this argument again here now, is he? "I'm private. You're not."

I've stunned him. "Me?" he says, pointing at himself. "Not private?"

Becca stares at my dad, then at me. Then at my dad again. No doubt she's thinking this is all very surreal.

"I am private, girly. I write lyrics because I have to, because it kills me if I don't, not so everyone can hear my thoughts. It's like . . . a need." He jots something down on one of his Post-Its.

A need. Please. E-mail is a need. Cable is a need. Becca just stands there real awkward, like a twelve-year-old boy at the Playboy Mansion.

"Come on, Becca. I'll show you the yard again."

"Thanks for what you've done," she blurts.

What's this?

Dad tilts his head. "What's that?"

For a second Becca looks like she's got nothing else to say. But then . . . "For giving me a reason to listen to music. Your songs, with all the crap out there, they actually mean something."

Please, when I meet my lifelong idol, remind me to use the word *crap*.

Dad's heard it all before, but still, he seems genuinely touched. "Why, thank you," he says gallantly, with a smile gorgeous enough to make even me a fan. "Thanks for saying that. You've made my day."

Oh, puh-leez! That should be Becca's line, Dad.

"I know this is stupid, but if Desert and I are gonna be friends, can I just get something out of my system?" Becca asks, kneading her fingers.

What now? Why do people insist on making fools of themselves in front of celebrities?

"Knock yourself out, sister," he says.

With confidence unknown to me, she strolls over to Dad, reaches out her hands, and pulls him to his feet. Then, listen to this, like a grown woman meeting her real father for the first time, she reaches around and hugs him. Hard. "Your songs"—she sniffs—"they've meant everything to me."

He does his best must-appreciate-my-fan hug then looks at me. I can just see those deer and bunnies in the woods starting to hold paws and sing gaily right about now. He smoothes down her hair. "Shh. I know, I know."

No, he doesn't, but whatever.

Normally my eyes would do a major roll at this point. But then something tells me Becca really, really needed this.

Chapter Nine

This woman is getting on my nerves. Since when does writing songs entail beaded bikinis and tanning oil? I swear you'd think that when we bought this house, Faith Adams came with it.

"Desert, honey, could you bring me a bottle of water, please? It's ridiculous hot out here!" *Ridiculous hot.* She can't even speak properly. She fans herself with her hand, like that'll help. Half an inch more and she'd be slapping herself in the face. Maybe if I just shoved her elbow . . .

"I was looking for my dad." *Not coming to take your order.* "Have you seen him?"

"He's in the studio, pup."

Pup? What the hell is that? I know this doesn't require a response. My die-Faith-die look should be enough. I walk past her and kick the pool water, pretending to be testing it. Some of it splashes on her pretty little feet.

She retracts her legs against her surgically enhanced body. "Hey! Careful there!"

"Woops, sorry."

No, I'm not. I rule!

"Desert," she calls out, "don't forget my water, please!"

Me Desert. Me no have water. You melt out here, Miss Silicon.

"Be right back," I answer. I've got no intention of returning whatsoever.

Can someone please explain why this is necessary? Why is it that whenever someone is working closely with my dad on a project, it's imperative they move in, forcing me to act all nice, like it's a pleasure having them around the whole time? Shouldn't they be the ones kissing my dad's butt, not the other way around?

It's only been two weeks since school started, and already, we have a day off. It's a Teachers' Planning Day. Or maybe it's Rosh Hashanah. Whatever. Marie and Mom went out for lunch, leaving me home with this tart. I didn't even know they were going anywhere. Otherwise I would've begged them to let me come along. Now I'm stuck.

"Hey, Dad. What's up?" I prop open the studio door and watch the spectacle inside. Dad's mad at paper. He's kicking sheets around, the rubber sole of his sneakers creasing and grinding them into the floor.

"Nothing," he mumbles.

"Yes, I can see that. Absolutely nothing is going on in here."

"Is your mother gone?"

"Yep. Lunch with Marie."

"Did she say where she was going?"

"Nope. But Faith is here!"

"Is she working on it?"

On what, her tan? Yeah, she's working on it all right. "Um . . . not sure what you're talking about, Dad. She's outside on the deck. Are you gonna be working for a while?"

"I'm not going anywhere until we get at least one good tune. J. C.'s on his way." Ah, yes. J. C.'s coming over. This means they'll be working until 6 A.M. without any sleep. He'll be in the zone for a while, and that means . . . The Jag awaits.

"Becca?" I switch my cell to the other ear, the wind whipping my ponytail in my face.

"Hey, Desert! What's up? I hardly slept last night. Couldn't stop thinking about your dad!"

"Right, whatever. Hey, wanna go to the Grove?"

"What do you mean? We live in the Grove."

"No, I mean, do you want to cruise around? I've got the car! Woo hoo!"

"The what? Car?"

"I'll be there in two minutes." *Beep.*

Becca's standing outside her house, looking like a mess. She waves at me like a goofball as I pull to a stop. I toss a scrunchie her way. Certainly one cannot cruise without one's proper cruising attire.

"You are *too* cool!" she cries, jumping in, and we take off flying, until the next speed bump anyway.

"Where do you want to go? I'll take you anywhere, baby!" She's staring at me like I'm the best thing ever.

"Like I care! This weekend's changed everything. We could go to Kmart, and that'd be fine. Just drive!"

What are we doing? I don't really know. Yes, I'm completely aware of the fact I have only a restricted license, a California one at that, and my dad has no idea I've hijacked his wheels. Let's just say Becca and I have this overwhelming need to get away today.

We drive to Miami Beach on this gorgeous Monday afternoon, checking out the cruise ships along the way. As we fly on McArthur Causeway to Watson Island, I catch Becca smiling blissfully, and I'm all too aware she's living out some kind of dream right here.

After an hour of sightseeing South Beach bodies, Art Deco buildings, and door after door of restaurants and clubs, we see a car leaving, so we snag its parking space. Trudging through the sand to find a nice spot on the beach, Becca unleashes the personal questions.

"So, what's it like? Being the daughter of the most famous rock god on the face of the earth?"

Oh, brother, here we go. "First of all, he's not the most famous rock god on the face of the earth. Second, he's not a god at all. . . . This is a good spot." We plop down.

"That's debatable." She laughs.

"Becca, take it from me. I admire my dad, but he's no god." *Did I just say I admire my dad?* "Anyway, to answer your question, it's mostly okay. Sometimes, though, I'm dying to know how other people live. Just normal, everyday people."

Becca does her little sniff-laugh, drawing a happy face in the sand, minus the smile. "Why? There's nothing interesting about the way other people live. They don't write E! True Hollywood Stories about people like me. You're the one with the cool life."

Sheesh, she doesn't get it. "It's not always cool. Take touring. It has its good and bad parts, but basically, I'm on the road half my life! I don't get to make friends the way you do. My friends are the people I see a few months at a time at school who do whatever they can to get backstage passes. See what I mean?"

Becca looks like she's going to ask for a backstage pass just to be funny, but I stop her with a pointed finger to her nose. "You can't get any more backstage than this, so don't even think about it, missy!"

"Okay!" she cries. "But you get to go places, see things, meet interesting people all the time, right?"

"Sometimes. I'll admit that's a plus. But then there's the press, the questions, the cameras, the lies being printed. It's not always peachy."

Becca leans back, hands burrowing into the sand. "I can't imagine. I just can't imagine what I'd do with your life."

"Ask for yours back. That's what you'd do. What about you? What's your story?" I ask, although Liam's already told me a good amount.

She stares out at the waves, the kids toting their sand castle kits, the joggers trampling by. "I know Liam's told you. Better him than me, since I don't like to talk about it. Don't get me wrong, I love my grandmother and everything, but it's not the same. I have no life. Sometimes, it sucks to the point where . . . I've even thought of ending it, you know?" She looks at me, shielding the glare from her eyes.

No. No, I don't know. "What do you mean? Why would you even think that?"

She sighs and gazes ahead. "Do you know what it's like to be invisible? You could disappear for a couple of days and no one would even care."

I think about this but don't respond. That's some serious moping going on right there.

"Look, I don't expect you to understand," she says, looking away. "It's complicated."

"Oh, sure, someone like me wouldn't understand, thanks!"

"No," she says, rethinking her comment. "What I mean is, most people don't understand it—not having anything to live for. I know this sounds crazy, but Crossfire's music is the only thing that keeps me going sometimes."

Wow. I've heard of people who find solace in music, live for it even, but didn't know they really existed. Kind of like fairies or something. Crossfire saving Becca from obliterating herself? Fine, I'll accept it. My dad's written some pretty great songs. Still, it's just music. I mean, come on.

I check my watch. Mom should be getting back soon, if she's

not home already, raising hell about the missing kid and car. "It's not crazy, Becca. Believe me, I get it. We gotta head back. Keep talking, though, I'm listening."

"Becca!" I shout, because one must shout to be heard in a moving convertible.

There's that smile again. That sorry, pained smile.

"What's the matter? Didn't you have a good time? I picked you up hoping we'd have fun!"

"Yeah, I did! This was awesome! I can't believe we did this!" She had fun, but not enough to wipe that look of self-pity off her face.

We come off the I-95 ramp onto US-1 and slow down at the first red light. One may stop screaming now. I turn to Becca. *"Oye, meng. Que pasa?"* I've learned much Spanglish in the cafeteria.

"I'm fine. I just know that my life won't ever be this way. That was a glimpse of your life."

"A what? A glimpse of my life? Um . . . hello, we just took a drive, that's all. What're you talking about?"

"Desert, c'mon. Nobody lives like this."

"Like what? We cruised around. Doesn't everyone our age cruise around for fun?"

"Yeah, but not in Jaguar convertibles, being stared at."

"So?" Geez, can you say party pooper?

"Nothing. It's just a painful reminder of where you'll still be dropping me off—my street, my crappy house, my crappy room, while you go off to—"

"Okay, enough already!" Next time I'll pick up Liam instead. He doesn't bitch nearly as much. Uh-oh. I forgot I said I'd call him this weekend.

"Sorry." She pulls off my scrunchie then rings it around the stick shift. "Desert, I just want you to know I won't be a leech to you, I promise."

Well, that's something nobody's ever said to me. "I never thought you would be, Becca. If I did, I never would've talked to you, or gone to your house, or picked you up. I did all those things 'cause I thought we were friends, not leeches. So stop feeling so damn sorry for yourself already!" I smile, and her face has a hint of genuine happiness in it for once.

We pull up to her house. "Now get out, you leech!"

She laughs, steps out, and closes the door. Then she leans into the car. "Thanks. This has been one hell of a weekend. I'm glad we're friends. Not 'cause of your dad, even though that's a major bonus, but because I always have a blast with you."

Looking depressed half the time is having a blast? "Same here, Beck. Oh, look, we're down to one-syllable names, see? That really means we're friends."

"That's right. Des," she says, with that face of hers. I guess that's just Becca for you, all mopey, all the time. "Later." She flashes me a peace sign.

On the drive home, I wonder about her. I wonder if maybe I didn't just get myself into something I shouldn't have. This is how it starts, you know, by telling people your secrets. Then your life's no longer your own. I hope she's right; I hope she's not a leech and I can trust her.

Pulling into the garage, I can see that Mom's not back yet, but J. C.'s car is here. I put the top back up and make sure everything's just as it was before I left. This little joyride was way too easy. Dad must really be absorbed by this album!

The garage entrance leads into the kitchen. Inside, I open the fridge and grab a diet Coke. I make it two. Dad never refuses 'em, and J. C. doesn't drink anything without the proper alcohol content. And Faith . . . well, who cares?

When I get to the studio door, I can hear jamming from inside. J. C.'s onto something with that funky riff. Dad's accompanying him on bass. It's making a lot of sense, except for the nasty voice as the third layer. I don't want to intrude, but with as much as they're into this, they probably won't even notice me, so I walk in.

You know how they say the devil takes many forms? Well, there's Faith, crooning some God-awful crap, but no, even better, she's singing in her freakin' bikini! Bouncing up and down, beads are flying, like she's really into the jam, but I'm sorry . . . any woman anywhere can see what she's doing.

I wait until they come to a break before announcing my arrival with, "Nice! I didn't know you guys already started working on the stage act."

Faith looks at me like she'd smack me with a flyswatter if she could. "We're not working on the stage act," she flat-out imitates me. "By the way, thanks for my water, Desert."

"Oh, I'm sorry, did I forget?"

On his stool, J. C. snickers behind his guitar. Dad greets me with a smile. "Is that for me, girly?"

I'm still holding the cold soda cans. "Yeah." I toss one over to him. "Sorry, J. C., I would've gotten you one. Didn't know you were here."

He smiles, cigarette dangling from his lip, and holds up his glass of vodka on the rocks for me to behold.

"Ah. Gotcha." I look over at Freak, Faith I mean, and make it a point to stare at her body for like, five whole seconds. That's what she wants, isn't it? For everyone to gawk at her boobs? I'll gawk.

"Yes?" she asks, like I didn't pay the twenty bucks for this peep show.

"Yes, what?"

You're in my house, supposedly working on a serious project, with two grown men giggling like four-year-olds at your Barbie-doll self, while my mother isn't home to watch over you, and all you can say to me is "Yes?" Give me one good reason why I shouldn't throw your sorry ass out the door!

God! How I'd love to actually say all that!

I don't have to. Faith looks over at Tweedle Dee and Tweedle Dum, rolls her eyes like the child here just doesn't get it, and pulls a full-length sundress out from her straw bag. She slips it on, with a sarcastic smile, and does a ta-da with her arms. "Happy?"

I won't waste words on her. I walk out and slam the door.

Great. How'd she do that? She's managed to make me feel like an ice princess. I've never been a prude, but still, is there any good reason for that ridiculous display? It's not as if Dad and J. C. are gonna ask her to cover up. I hate this! Feeling like a patrol guard, keeping the so-called adults in line. I'm sick of it! What would've happened if I hadn't interrupted? Free lap dances for everyone?

Heading upstairs, my stomach hurts. I slam the door shut and yank out a sheet of paper from my notebook. I throw myself onto the bed.

> Intruder alert, who can this be?
> New member of the family?
> I swear to God, if she does stay
> It's me that will be going away
> I cannot take it; I can't ignore
> The desert just inside the door
> I want out now, please let me go
> To places where the waters flow.

Look, I ain't going for a Nobel Prize, all right? Whatever. . . .

Chapter Ten

Right as I finish my homework, and I'm about to settle into bed, Mom knocks on the door, hard. "Desert, open up."

Yikes. She hasn't come out of her room since she got home with Marie, but now she wants to talk to me? As I'm about to doze off? Super timing. I hope it's nothing major. I have to get up early for school tomorrow.

"Come in, it's unlocked!" I shout across the room.

The door opens, and there stands my mom, ponytail all limp, loose hair strands around her face, dark circles under her eyes. I would've expected her to look this way tomorrow, considering they're about to have an all-night rehearsal with J. C., but now?

"What's up?" I ask.

"Desert, what'd you do today?"

Ugh. The question. It means she knows the answer, she's just giving me a head start before hunting and shooting me down. How does she always figure me out?

"Um . . . went to the beach with Becca?" No more, no less.

"Oh, yeah?" she asks with a hint of sadness, like she's yet to see the beach since we moved.

"Yeah. Why do you ask?"

She leans onto the door frame and sighs. "Des, honey, listen. There's a lot going on right now with the recording and all . . . your father's stressed, I'm stressed."

I remember Dad and J. C. earlier today, giggling at the G-string Wonder, looking anything but stressed. "He is? He didn't look it this afternoon."

"Desert, I don't care how he looked or anything you might've seen, okay. All I came to tell you was I have enough going on right now, between the sessions, the move, the paparazzi, the hiring of new help, promoters who are still hassling me about last year's deals, Marie going home for a couple of weeks—"

"Marie left? In the middle of recording?"

She goes on, ignoring me, "Without having to find sand in your father's car, along with this!" She flings my scrunchie at me.

Oops.

"Hey, my scrunchie! Where'd you find it?" I ask all innocent, smiling my fakest smile ever.

She points a finger at me and starts wiggling it around. "Drop the act, okay? The next time I find out you've taken that car, *any* car, with or without a license, without my permission, you can forget about getting one for your birthday. Do you hear me?"

Do you hear me? God, I hate when she says that! Of course I hear you, how stupid! I have to remember never to ask my kids that question when I'm a parent. But hey, if this is all the punishment I'm getting, I'll happily comply. "Yes, Mom," I force out.

"Good," she growls. "Good night."

"Good night." Door closes.

That's it? How totally weird! That wasn't too bad. I guess she really does have a lot on her mind.

Chapter Eleven

Is it me, or are people staring? I've gotten way too used to the wonderful sense of anonymity in these halls, but now Trumpet Kid and Flute Girl right there just eyed me. Quick glances, not like my gawking at Faith yesterday, but definitely making eye contact.

At my locker Becca catches up and shoulders me softly. "Hey, you."

I see she's wearing eyeliner. Impressive. "Hi. I tried calling you last night, but nobody answered."

"Yeah, we were having dinner at Didi's."

"Didi!" I laugh. "Why do I picture someone with poofy white hair and leathery skin?"

From Becca's frozen face, I'd say I'm not too far off with that description. "Hey, don't make fun of poor Didi! She works real hard to get her hair to puff up like that."

"Wow, I was right? You gotta introduce me to her. She sounds smashing, baby."

"She is," Becca says with a laugh. "Did you do your English homework?"

Did I do my English homework? "Of course I did. Why? Didn't you?" *Too busy reanalyzing all of Flesh's lyrics last night, now that you're one with him?*

"Yeah, I did, but first I needed some inspiration." She pulls out a Crossfire CD insert from the front pocket of her bookbag and starts reading aloud some of Dad's phenomenal lines.

"Good lord, Becca. Put that away."

"What do you think your dad meant by 'The melody calls, it beckons and falls, its rhythm explodes, my body—it holds'?"

Some kid with geeky hair just looked at me too. "I think he meant for you to read it over and over until you're completely crazy."

"I think he was probably experiencing some sort of temptation, from the sound of it, don't you?"

"Whatever, dude. Think whatever you wanna think, Beck. That's why he's called an artist."

We head off toward first period. The hallway's packed with students going through their morning routines. Something's slightly off. Are people whispering?

"Rain forest."

"Mountain," someone says in a tiny voice as two skinny kids whisk past me.

"Did you hear what those jerks just said to me?" I turn around quickly, only to see the idiots disappear around the corner laughing.

"No, what'd they say?" Becca asks.

"Nothing, forget it." Yes, I'm definitely drawing attention. Did I put clothes on this morning? Becca wouldn't have blabbed already, would she?

For a few seconds Room 214 falls silent when we walk in. Then the chatter starts up again as Ms. Smigla comes around, collecting our homework. She nabs my crappy poems, glances at them, and looks up with a grin. She either likes my writing or my name still amuses her. Either way, she says nothing. Very unlike Smig.

Liam rushes in just as the bell rings and looks over at me quickly. I can't quite read his expression, but there's no smile today. I was going to call him last night, but after dealing with Faith yesterday, I was in a pretty sour mood. Now he'll probably think I'm not the least bit interested. I should've called!

Ms. Smigla begins class by reading through the poems without mentioning anyone's name. She pretends to like them all, hard to believe, but I know she's trying to encourage everyone's creativity. You can tell the ones she really likes from the way she stops and dwells in discussion.

"'Will you cast stones at what you perceive?'" she asks the class in that melodramatic way of hers.

My ears perk up.

"Interesting parallel to someone significant. Anyone know to whom this poem refers?" She looks up, searching for an answer.

Nobody grabs this one. It's a case of "Anyone? Anyone? Bueller?" from that *Ferris* movie, but there are no takers, just a couple of coughs. Oh, for crying out loud. Jesus! Jesus Christ! Doesn't anyone watch the History Channel?

Liam raises his hand. Ms. Smigla happily calls on him. "That's about that prostitute in the Bible, when everyone wants to stone her. But Jesus makes them all feel guilty."

Yes! And the points keep pouring in for Liam Blanco!

"That's right. Someone here feels persecuted," Ms. Smigla says, glancing around.

If she looks directly at me, I will personally see to *her* crucifixion. Lucky for her, she doesn't. She then adds, "I suppose we all do sometimes." She goes on to the next poem.

Kuntz glances over. Kuntz has always been in his own little world over there. Weird that he would suddenly notice me. But then Pigtails glances over. Pigtails has never shown me her face. All right, enough. I know what's going on here. My pen scribbles like mad.

who did you tell?

I push the scrap onto Becca's desk.

She reads it and gives me a quizzical look. Then she writes something and hands it back.

What are you talking about?

Why would everyone be staring at me today unless you said something??!!

I haven't said anything!!! I swore I wouldn't!

Then tell me why people have been giving me weird looks today!

How the hell should I know??

Well, if it wasn't her, then who was it? Nobody knows but her!

Nobody knows but you

Becca reads this and pauses, faking attention to Ms. Smigla. Then, she jots down:

That you know of.

She turns up her palm and shrugs. Ms. Smigla gives us a warning look.

She's right. Maybe someone finally checked the Crossfire fansite and saw my name in Dad's bio. Damn. Well, what did I expect? If everyone knows about me, then fine, I can pass right through the initial shock phase and move on with my life. Becca took it well, right? We're still friends. The only thing is, I was hoping to know Liam better before the beans were spilled.

Liam does not turn around the entire fifty-five minutes of Smigla's lecture. When the bell rings, I'll just go over and explain that I was really busy unpacking this weekend and had things to do. He'll understand. Then I'll definitely call him tonight. That'll get the message through to him.

The bell eventually rings, and Liam bolts from his seat and out the door. Not a hello, a smile, a request for an explanation, nothing. Did he really expect me to swoon all over him after knowing each other for one day? *Go on, Liam, get out of here! Run off to your next class! Look, you even left your stupid disc case again.*

Next class? Great, next period is physics with Liam. Aurelio, the guy that sits next to him in this class, holds up the abandoned black case. "Anybody see Liam next period?"

I'm walking out of the same aisle, so I snatch it up. "I do. Gimme."

This is turning out to be a lovely day.

Becca meets me by the door and begins, "Desert, I would never tell anyone what you told me, okay? Why? Who's giving you weird looks?" She follows me down the hall, toward the science wing.

"Everyone."

"Like who?"

"Like people I don't even know." *Just leave me alone.*

"Well, is there some way maybe someone else knows about you? I mean, you yourself said that your name's on a bunch of websites, maybe someone saw it, maybe someone—"

"Maybe." *Go the hell away.*

"Desert, you don't really think it was me, do you?"

I stop and face her. "I don't know what to think, okay? Just . . . go to class. I'll see you later."

"Desert?" She stands there, confused and hurt, as I walk off. She just doesn't get it. She doesn't understand what this is like, what a bane to my freakin' existence it is to have this celebrity bullshit hanging over my head!

At the end of the hall, there's a crowd buzzing. They're facing the wall, looking up at something. I need to get through. "Excuse me." *Dammit, people, move!*

"That's her," someone says.

I look up to see all eyes on me. Those aren't grades on the bulletin board everyone's gaping at. They're photos. Of me and Dad.

Chapter Twelve

Remember that madness I said would start soon—the one where everybody changes once they know who I'm tied to? Well, it's here.

"Hey, is that you in those pictures?"

"That guy said you're Flesh's daughter. That true?"

"Dude, that's so awesome!"

"Did you hear that?"

"What girl?"

"This girl, this one."

"Ask her!"

"How come you're at our school? You guys live here?"

"Have you always gone to school here? I never knew that!"

"Bro, who the hell's Flesh?"

All these people are in my face, curious and dumbstruck. They're not trying to annoy the hell out of me, yet they've managed to. . . . I didn't wake up expecting this today or I might've worn something a little more presentable.

"Excuse me. Excuse me, please." This hallway is starting to swirl, it's so damn hot in here.

"Desert McGraw, man. I have sixth period with her."

"Who is she? What's the big deal, bro?"

All right, enough already. "Look," I say, stopping to face the clueless mob, "I'd appreciate it if you didn't talk about me like I wasn't standing right here."

The crowd gasps and leans back. The angry, caged animal is speaking to them.

"Hey, sorry," says a guy with red-tipped black hair and three earrings on each lobe. "We just didn't know you came to our school. That's cool."

I manage a sympathetic smile for these people while taking off to class. "Well, now you know."

"My name's Eddie!" he calls after me, and other people buzz around him to find out what I'd said.

Eddie, like I care. Did he ever introduce himself before he saw my dad on the board? No, I don't think so. I just wanna know one thing: Dammit, where's my stupid class again? There. Does Liam know anything? Probably. That's why he's not talking to me. I have to get to him before the others do. The bell's about to ring.

Inside the classroom everyone's chatting in small groups. They pause when they see me, and two guys actually start clapping.

Liam's not here and, honestly, I don't feel like being here either. I'm gone. If the teacher says anything, I think I have a pretty legitimate excuse for wanting privacy for a day.

I whirl right back around and exit before Mr. Borrel has a chance to catch me leaving. The bell rings, and the last of the stragglers shuffle in. The noise level in the room has gone up, making the empty hallway the perfect place to be.

Okay, think, Desert. What now? Do you go back in there, face everybody's questions with grace, or do you take a breather somewhere? I decide to take a breather.

First things first. I march over to the language wing bulletin board, where several kids are walking away, questioning each other about the display. I stop and stare for myself. Four photos of me getting home Friday, with my dad in the background picking up the newspaper. *How the hell did these get here?* I start unpinning them.

"Hey." Liam is behind me.

"Hey." I spin around, my heart practically in my throat. "What're you doing here?"

At first he says nothing. His long, dark eyelashes bat softly over those baby blues. Then "I was coming to take these down."

"Why? What do you care?" My face is creepier than ever, I can feel it, but I don't care. He's barely even looked at me today.

"I thought maybe you didn't want everybody seeing them?" he questions, like I should've guessed.

Duh. I must look like a bat out of hell, because he turns around to leave me standing there, photos in hand.

"Wait, Liam." My hand goes out to his shoulder. "Can I talk to you somewhere?"

"We should be in class." He tries escaping, but I stop him.

"Forget class. This is more important."

"What do you want to talk about?"

"These." I hold up a photo.

"I already know about that. Everyone does."

"But can I explain?"

"There's nothing to explain, Desert. You have every right to your privacy. You don't have to be sorry."

"I'm not sorry! I just want to explain it, to you, so you'll hear it from me, not anyone else."

"I already told you I know." He pauses, looking down at his hands. "I knew it before anyone else."

Excuse me? "Huh?"

"I found out Friday, okay?" His eyebrows shoot up, blue eyes looking guilty as all hell.

He has *got* to be kidding me! "No, it's not okay! What do you mean? How did you find out?"

He hesitates. . . . "Let's go. I'll explain everything."

"You found out Friday?" *The day we first talked?* "And you didn't say anything to me about it?" Great! This is just what I should've expected! Shame on me for thinking I could get away with this. For thinking anyone could like me for myself.

"Hey, listen," he says, holding his palms out, like he's got nothing to lose. "I don't know why you're so upset; you never said anything either, all right?"

I don't believe this! So he doesn't like me for me? It was all an act to get to know Flesh's daughter? *Beautiful, honey-eyed, interesting.* Dammit. Argghh! My hand slams the bulletin board, pushpins popping to the tile floor. "Liam!"

"What?"

A teacher sticks his head out the door and shushes us.

"It's nothing, forget it." *Just walk away, Desert. Go home, even.*

"Aren't you even the least bit interested in how I know about you?"

"Not really. Leave me alone." I wasn't ready for this. How stupid of me for thinking I could even pretend to have a normal life here! I'm leaving.

"My stepmother's a journalist."

I stop in my tracks, then do a one-eighty. "Excuse me?"

"Adriana Portilla. She writes for *Tropical Home Life.*"

"What is that?"

"A magazine down here."

"You mean a tabloid?" Great. My love interest is linked to a local tabloid. This is like some sick, twisted joke. "That's just fantastic!" I throw my arms up. I have nothing left to say.

"It's not a tabloid. Please . . ." He puts his hands up, as if I were armed. "Let's go somewhere to talk."

"Oh, now you wanna talk, do you?"

Liam steps back.

Backstage in the auditorium is the perfect place for me to murder Liam Blanco without anyone hearing so much as a peep.

How gallant of him to pull up a bucket for me to sit on. Oh, wait, it's for him. He offers me the only chair in sight.

"Just calm down, will you?"

Now I understand why Becca wanted to beat the crap out of me the other day. "Stop telling me to calm down! You listen to me . . . buddy!"

"Buddy?" he blurts, a smile brewing at the corner of his lips.

"Oh, so now you think this is funny?" I swear to God, if he laughs I'll kick his butt.

He's shaking his head, holding his nose at the same time, using all his powers not to laugh. Then he can't help it, and it all comes rolling out.

Son of a . . . *Smack!*

His cheek is stinging red, hand coming up to soothe the mark. Damn, I branded him.

"Oh! Oh, God! Liam! I'm sorry! I'm so sorry!"

But then he starts again, laughing harder, harder, and then some more. This isn't funny. This is serious, not something we can just ha-ha about, this is—okay, it's kinda funny. And suddenly I'm laughing too. Harder than him, I think. His cackles are feeding my hoots and vice versa. Is that me, snorting? This is what happens under great stress, isn't it? You just fall apart like this?

After a minute I say, "Okay, breathe." *Hold yourself, Des.* Liam's smile is more gorgeous than ever. It's just too bad I'm going to have to send him to hell now. "One chance. You explain. I'll listen."

Liam stretches out, taking a deep breath. "Ahhhhh." He looks up at the tall, dusty curtains, down at the wooden floor.

"I'm waiting." My nails tap the side of the aluminum chair.

"All right, look. My stepmom writes articles—"

"You mentioned that, Liam. Tell me something I don't know."

"I'm—give me a chance, will you?"

"Fine."

"Damn, girl! *Coño!*" he says, rolling his eyes.

Con-yo? Whatever that is, I guess I can be a pretty big pain in the ass.

"She writes a segment every month called Florida Families—kind of a look at different people and the way they live in South Florida. Sometimes it's good things. Sometimes . . . it's not." He looks at me and waits for my reaction.

"Mmm-hmm."

"Anyway . . ."

"You live with her?"

"On some weekends, but the rest of the time I live with my mom and Michael. My dad, my half sisters, and Adriana live in the Gables. *Anyway* . . ."

Maybe I should stop interrupting him.

"Someone tipped her off that Flesh and his family were moving to Miami and that your mom is gungho about managing the band to the point where she may be"—he pauses to hook his fingers as quotation marks—"'neglecting her daughter's needs.' So of course, Adriana jumped on the chance to write a killer story."

"A killer story? That would totally make my mom look like a bitch."

91

"I know. I'm sorry. But hey, that's journalism. *You* know that. She's just doing her job."

"Yeah, typical. Entertainment at the expense of others."

He smirks. "She has an aggressive style, especially toward families that are *different*. From everything that's ever been printed, it seems like yours handles everything so perfectly. And there's nothing Adri would love more than to prove everyone wrong."

"Whatever. I'm sure some journalists are just 'doing their job,' but I think a lot of them are just bitter and find it easier to make targets of nice people instead. Especially if the targets happen to be famous."

Liam shrugs. "Well, you might be right. The one thing I never liked about her—please don't tell my dad . . ."

I laugh. "I don't even know your dad!"

"Is that Adriana's always on this high horse about the virtues of motherhood and working from home while raising kids and all that, so it doesn't surprise me that she wants to do a piece on your mom. She figures it'd be interesting."

"Interesting, huh? So you think it's *interesting* that people read about my family's personal life while flipping through *Tropical Home Life* while sitting on the toilet? 'Cause that's all it is, Liam. Fodder."

I love that word.

"Yeah, well, I never said I agreed with it."

I look away. I hate this. Why do these problems follow me everywhere? "So how do you fit into this, Liam?"

He sighs and goes on. "She wants to know more about you, what you're like. If she can show that you behave irrationally, get along poorly with peers, and so on, then she's got more crap on your mom."

"What? So wait . . . she asked you to watch me, in case I act irrational? God, how totally ridiculous!"

He feels the slap mark on his face. "Yeah, how totally inconceivable."

Ugh. My head drops. "Well, isn't that nice?" I slide my hand along the curtain ropes next to me. Then I look at the pictures poking out of my backpack. "I had a stalker all along."

"Desert, I didn't take those shots. I didn't even know about them until after they were taken."

"Whatever."

"I didn't! I found out Friday night."

Friday night? So, he *did* pair up with me in class because he wanted to get to know me? *Hmm.*

As the corners of my eyes tear up, he goes on, "I know who set up the shot, but it wasn't me, I swear."

"You know? Who, Liam? Who hired the guy? Tell me!"

"I can't. Just listen to me. This is what I wanted to say—"

"What, you have more to tell me? Great, a man of many words!"

"Desert, just listen. I'm supposed to be watching you for Adri—"

"You mean *stalking* me for Adri."

"But Becca told me 'she's so cool, she's so funny,' telling me all about you—"

"Oh, so Becca knew all along too?" She's gonna pay for this!

"No, I haven't told her."

"Why not? She's Crossfire's biggest fan."

"Believe me, I was dying to all weekend, but I swore to Adri I wouldn't tell anyone while she was still getting her facts. But listen . . . I don't think I can do it, Desert. When we hung out on Friday, I thought you were extremely cool."

Stop it. Stop staring at me, Liam Blanco. You're very dangerous.

"And I started liking you before Adri asked me any favors."

No fair. If he thinks this is having no effect on me, then he doesn't know me at all. Why am I crying?

"I don't want to hurt you."

I wipe the stupid tears from my eyes. "Wait. Let me think about this. First you ignore me during English, then you won't tell me who parked outside my house and took my picture, but you don't want to hurt me either? Liam, if you don't want to hurt me, then say who took them! And who the hell posted 'em?"

His face twists in misery. I know I'm asking him to choose sides here, but I need to know where he stands. He may still be able to prove himself my friend.

"I don't know who posted them. Whoever found my CD case, probably. I left it on top of Michael's car this morning by mistake. When I went back to get it, it was open and the photos were gone."

"You mean to tell me these are yours?" I pull out the fantastic shots of me flicking my middle finger. This just keeps getting better and better!

94

"A photographer for the magazine took them and e-mailed copies to my stepmother, and she forwarded them to me so I could be sure who to look out for, since I didn't stay with her last weekend. I only brought them to school because I wanted to ask you about it. I'm really sorry, Desert. I wasn't gonna show them to anyone."

I raise a McGraw eyebrow at him.

"Well, Becca, if anyone, but I didn't. I shouldn't have kept them in that stupid case. I'm always leaving it everywhere."

I reach into my bag and pull out his CD case. Then I chuck it at him. "Why don't you glue the damn thing to your butt, so you don't lose it?"

He rolls his eyes and sighs. Then he smiles. Liam finds the most awkward moments to show his sense of humor.

I think about all this for a minute. So my pictures went up. So what? I just wasn't expecting the secret to get out like this. As my dad would say, "Get on with life, girly."

"All right," I finally say, exhaling loudly. "Fine. But just tell me who hired the guy and let's forget about this."

He exhales deeply, then takes my hands in his. They're big and warm and feel really, really nice around mine. I have this overwhelming urge to forgive everything, but if he knows this much, he better tell me now, or else William White is history.

"Someone named Marie."

Chapter Thirteen

Demons walk among us, demons in the air
Devil's children, posing playmates
Lurking, hiding everywhere
Tell me it wasn't you, tell me I can breathe
Easier now, you wouldn't do this to me
Would you, dear? Would you turn?
Would you betray without concern?
Will we ever come to learn?
Just one chance, explain to me
Your place within this family tree
Our trust in you, in jeopardy

From: saharagobi@crossfire.com
To: "Brianna Roman"
Subject: Phys Ed

this week's been the pits. situation here's getting desperate, not like u give a rat's ass. since u never leave ur computer, i'm gonna assume uv bailed on me, so there's no point in calling to see where the hell uv been. Unless ur connection's been down for a month, in which case, sorry. i thought we were friends. guess i was wrong. i guess u don't need anybody, now that u finally got ur implants. by the way, don't trust anyone with ur little secret, or u'll be out of st. alf in a heartbeat. in fact, don't trust anyone, period.

—des

Chapter Fourteen

Since Liam told me about Marie two weeks ago, I haven't said anything to anybody. First of all, since she went home, she's not here to defend herself, and second, I'm not sure how I'm supposed to tell my parents that our very own right hand may be exposing us. But I guess I have to talk to my mom at some point. Time to test the waters . . .

On the deck my mother sits on a lounge chair, facing the bay. I can see her cigarette smoke quickly blowing away in the breezy night air. The full moon lights up her face, making her tears sparkle. She didn't hear me come outside. When she sees me, she swipes her cheeks, then nervously grinds out the stub of her cigarette.

"Sweetie . . . I was . . . it's only—"

"A cigarette, Mom. Don't worry. I won't tell Dad."

A halfhearted smile appears, then she reaches for my hand, pulling me to join her brooding session. I settle alongside her, curling up like a little kid. It feels kind of weird. We haven't sat like this in years. But almost immediately it feels familiar again.

Mom doesn't cry a whole lot, so when she does it's a big deal. Either she's pissed at Dad, or . . . she's pissed at Dad. They never argue in front of me, so I can never know for sure. Unless she's crying.

"You guys at it?" I ask, tucking my hair into the back of my T-shirt to keep it out of my face.

She stares at the water, swishing softly in the moonlight, and nods. Then she bites her lip, like she's going to lose it.

If this is about Faith, I swear I'll rearrange her face. "Mom, what is it?"

She shakes her head. "Nothing, honey. Just a fight. It happens."

Yeah, about a blond freak of nature, I bet. Why don't they fire her already? "A fight about Faith?" I ask.

Her eyes perk up. "Faith? Why would you say that?"

Guess not. "Nothing. I just see the way she carries on with Dad and J. C. I thought maybe those short shorts of hers have pissed you off for the last time."

She lights up a new cigarette, hand trembling. "No, honey. It's not Faith. Don't worry, I'll be fine." Lips pressed together, she fights back a sob. Yes, I can see she'll be just fine.

Could it be about Marie? Does Mom know what Liam told

me? Does Liam even have the right info? How do I ask her? *C'mon, Desert, she's your mom, just come right out with it.* "Mom?"

"Mmm?"

"Is something going on I don't know about?"

She snorts, meaning I don't know the half of it. "Desert, honey, lots of things go on you don't know about."

No kidding. And I spend half my time trying to figure them out. "I heard something a couple weeks ago."

She looks down at her tissue, unfolding and refolding it. "If it was printed, then it's not true."

"No, it wasn't printed. A kid at school knows who took the pictures. Someone working for a local writer named Adriana. Portilla, or something."

I wait for her eyes to widen, the spark of surprise to appear on her face, but she just smiles softly. "I know."

Am I the only idiot this side of the Mississippi? I straighten up, sitting on the edge of the lounge chair. "You do? How?"

She side glances me like I should know the obvious answer to that. "Marie got the scoop, hon."

"Oh."

I get it. Marie told her herself, so it wouldn't look like she's involved. Like she found out through a third party, then informed Mom, as any good little assistant would do. Tricky. Let's see how much Marie actually told her. "But do you know who tipped them off that we're living here?"

"No, and I don't care. It was going to happen sooner or later. Where'd you hear about the reporter, Des?"

"From this guy at school—a kid named Liam." I get up and walk to the railing, looking down at the surf breaking below. The wind swoops my hair right out of my shirt. "He's her stepson."

"Really?"

This much she didn't know. I can see that. I face her and nod.

"And you're seeing him?" she asks, eyebrows drawn together.

"Seeing?" I ask. "We like each other, we hang out a lot, but we're not dating, if that's what you mean. We're just friends." How did she change the subject like that? I'm here to fish for Marie info, not discuss boyfriend possibilities.

"Just be careful please, Desert."

Here we go.

"He might be using you to get to me," she says. "To us."

And I thought she was launching into the "Be careful you don't get pregnant" speech. Lovely. "Mom, don't start with all that—"

Her palm flies up to stop me. "Honey, think. If he's related to her, then he may not"—she pauses for the right way of putting it—"care about you."

"Not care about me?"

"You know what I mean, Desert. Yes, believe it or not, there are people who want to get close to us who don't care about us."

They say sarcasm runs in the family.

I've never thought for one second that Liam may not care about me. Okay, maybe half of a second. "Mom, listen to me, all right? I can't keep going around not trusting people all the time! I have to make some friends!"

"Yes, I know, but you still have to be careful."

"I am careful! What do you want me to do, get a full background check on everyone I meet?"

"Desert," she says in a tone that means keep my sass to a minimum. "You can't trust anyone you just met in school, okay? Especially someone related to a tabloid reporter!"

"Really?" I can't believe this lecture. "I don't think *you* should be telling *me* who I should and shouldn't trust, Mom!"

She squints at me and tilts her head. "What's that supposed to mean?"

Oops. I guess she really doesn't know anything about Marie and the photos. Plus there's still the chance that Marie hasn't done anything wrong. *Brush it off, Des.* "Nothing, forget it."

She folds her tissue until it's a tiny, white block. "Look . . . honey, the only people you can fully trust are your dad and me."

"That's not good enough!" *Why am I shouting?* "I need friends, Mom. Real friends! You guys won't be around forever!"

Her face hardens, as if she never realized I thought about things like that, then looks away, fist at her mouth. "Sweetie, all I meant was watch your back, okay?"

"I do, Mother! I try, but I can't watch my back to the point where I'm freakin' paranoid!" I can't believe she's asking *me* to be careful when Marie might be stabbing us in the back! "Don't you think I'm capable of choosing my friends?"

Her tears are building up again. "Of course I do!" she cries, flinging one away with her thumb. "Desert, don't be so naïve, for God's sake! Our situation is different, not normal, as much as you'd like it to be! Would you just think for a minute?"

"I am thinking!" My voice just shot up about fifty decibels more. "Don't you think I think about things? Don't you think I'm tired of dealing with all this? I wish my life was like anybody else's! I wish I could watch TRL without seeing my dad come onto the set!" I push myself off the railing and head back to the house.

God, I hate her! She can be so damn infuriating! Sorry, God, sorry. I don't hate her.

"Sweetie," she implores, grabbing my arm as I rush past her, "this has been a horrific week, with the sessions and all. The last person I need to argue with now is you."

Yeah, well then, why bother? But of course, I don't say it.

"I'm sorry," she says. "I do trust your judgment."

"Whatever. Just forget it." *That* conversation went well. I pull out of her grip and start up the path.

Funny, even with my mom, who I trust more than anyone, warning me about Liam . . . it's him I feel like running to now. Even if she's right. Even if he is using me.

On Friday nights, the Grove is crazy packed, but if you know the hideouts, like Liam does, there are some nice places to hang out. At first I thought this was a park like any other. Hard to tell with the dim streetlights. But now I see it's a cemetery. As goth as it may sound, the iron gates, gazillion trees, and crickets chirping actually make it very beautiful. Especially with the full moon out.

Liam sits cross-legged on an old bench, an arm draped over the back. Next to him, I listen to the soft drone of his voice, sliding my scrunchie on and off my wrist.

"He swears he's happy with Adri, but then, why the drinking, you know?"

"It just started?" I ask.

"Nah, he's been doing it for years, but never when he was with my mom."

"Maybe that's why they split. Maybe he got sloshed in private, and you just didn't know anything."

"No, you don't know my dad. He never would've drank in private. They didn't even argue in private. Michael, Carrie, and I had the pleasure of hearing every word. You know how hard it is to watch the Cartoon Network with your dad calling your mom a bitch in the next room?"

Sister? "Wait . . . how many brothers and sisters do you have?" I ask. This is getting confusing. Maybe couples should only be allowed one child, like I heard they do in China.

"Well, there's me, Michael, and my sister, Carrie, from my mom and dad's marriage. Carrie's nineteen. She goes to UM . . . lives in the dorm. Then there're our little half sisters, Carolina and Lilian, who are still in elementary school."

"Wow."

"I know, the true meaning of 'extended family.' So yeah, my dad's always been like that. But he's still a good person, though." Liam looks off somewhere.

"That sucks," I offer. I'm trying to imagine Liam as a little kid, listening to his parents fight over who contributes more to the marriage or who's more underappreciated.

"You get used to it after a while. No big deal."

He's lying. It was a big deal. I can see it all over his face. In sympathy, I punch his sneaker playfully.

"Whatever." He sighs. "Everybody's got a vice, right? Some people beat their kids. Some people can't tell the truth to save their lives. My dad's is alcohol."

"I guess that's true," I say. I had never thought of that before. What's my vice? Leaving my mom behind when she most needs someone to talk to?

"So, that's my story. Nice, huh?"

"Listen, everybody's got screwed-up people in their family." *Oops.* "Not that your dad is screwed up; what I mean is nobody's perfect." *Nice save, Des.*

There's that grin of his. My stomach quivers. If I had a camera, I'd take a shot of him just like that, with his hand over his knee in those jeans. "Yeah, nobody's perfect," he says, "but some people come closer than others."

Like you, Liam Blanco. You're pretty damn close to perfect. "Well, that's a given," I say instead, but I almost lost myself thinking of what it would be like to hold that sweet face and taste those lips . . .

"What about you?" he asks, scratching off spray paint from the bench's ironwork. My mental image fades to black. "Everything okay with the Crossfire family?"

Actually, everybody in the band can be pretty messed up sometimes, but I guess I don't have too much crap to report on my folks. They argue like anybody else's parents. Big deal.

"They go through phases," I say. "Sometimes things are incredible, usually when a set is released, and the reviews are good. Everybody celebrates. It's a great time. But the recording months aren't always smooth. The band used to work well together, but lately, some people, whose names I won't mention"—*Max* and *Phil*—"don't work as hard as my parents do. And that makes everybody tense, know what I mean?"

He nods. "Yep. Not doing their part, and the rest pick up their slack?"

"Right. Don't get me wrong, I love them, everybody. Crossfire really is a family, but they split apart at times. And now they think they need an outsider to help them develop an updated sound, so I can't help but figure things'll end soon."

Maybe I'm telling him too much. *Yes, too much, Desert, slow down.* I can just see my mother shaking her disappointed head a mile from here.

"Wow. Crossfire breaking up?" he asks, inspecting a piece of peeled paint. "They've been around forever."

"I know, right?"

"How long? Like fifteen years?"

"Seventeen."

"Damn."

"Yeah, and if that happens, I might finally get to call one place home," I tell him.

And then, somewhere in my brain, I hear a *ding*.

Why didn't I think of this before? If Faith's lyrical input contributes to a Crossfire breakup, then maybe having her around isn't such a bad thing. Dad's already stressed from not getting a decent tune out of her. Mom's crying over God knows what. Marie might be sabotaging us, although that's still unconfirmed. Put it all together, and I may just get my normal life after all! And here I was seeing everything all back-asswards!

And you know what? I might know another way to get this disbanding thing going a little faster. "Liam?"

"Desert?"

Too funny. "Liam?"

"Desert?"

Good Lord. "You know what?"

"Chicken butt."

"Excuse me?"

He laughs. "You never saw that episode on *SNL* where the guy asks, 'What?' and every time he does, the other guy would say, 'Chicken butt'?"

I'll let my face do the talking on this one.

"Okay, forget it. What were you gonna say?" he asks.

"What I was *gonna* say is, your stepmom is looking for crap for her article, right?"

"Not crap, exactly."

"Your words, Liam."

"Evidence, I meant."

Evidence. And evidence paired with a psychologist's analysis about my need for stability equals my mom finally understanding she's been wrong, that it's time to raise the kid in a permanent home environment. So that just leaves one thing.

"Give her what she wants then," I say.

"What?"

"You heard me. Tell her I'm completely unstable."

"Don't be ridiculous!"

"Pardonnez-moi?"

"I said don't *be* ridiculous, not that you are, Des. Why would you want people to think that? You're a totally cool person. Amazing. Not unstable."

"Thanks, Liam." *Tell me how you really feel!* "But my mom won't care. She won't! She's used to stuff like this being printed. She ignores it for the most part but is definitely used to it. 'Ignore criticism' has always been her attitude."

"Then why do this?" he asks, and I can see the worry all over his face.

"Because! Let's see, where do I even begin? Do you have any idea what it's like to call a bus your home? To not have one place to grow up? To not have the same friends year after year? To always have to follow a plan, an itinerary? There's no room for being spontaneous, to just say, 'Hey Mom, can we go to the movies today?' It's little things like that I want more than anything. An article about my mother would just be one more straw on the camel's back!"

"One more what?"

"You never heard that saying? The whole thing about the camel's back? God, I spend too much time around old farts. That's another problem. Just do it. Tell Adriana what she wants to hear. Tell her I'm a real freak."

"But you're not!"

"Liam, I know what I'm doing."

I can tell he doesn't like the idea. "Fine. I'll think of something, not because I want to. It won't be easy. 'Cause you're not, you know," he says, leaning in and taking my hands again in his. "You're not."

Let me just say, these strong hands have kept my mind awake every night this week. I can't even tell you the places I've imagined them. All I know is, he's got me crazy, like when we're on the phone together. And from the way he's eyeing my mouth, I think I'm getting something else to keep my thoughts busy for another week.

"I'm not?" I ask, almost forgetting the last thing he said.

"No. You're beautiful." He pushes a strand of hair away from my face. "And sweet as hell," he adds, tucking it behind my ear. Holding my chin, he caresses my lip with his thumb, bringing his mouth in slowly. "And I'll do anything you ask me, Desert McGraw."

Gulp.

"If you'll just let me kiss you."

Chapter Fifteen

The memory of our kiss has been distracting me for two days. But now Marie's back. And as soon as she walks into the house, I kidnap her and make her drive us to CocoWalk.

"Is it true?" I ask, slurping down what's left of my cookies 'n' cream shake. She better say no.

"Is what true, Desi?" Marie asks, eyelid twitching. She finishes off the last of her curly fries without as much as a glance my way. Something is up.

Once I saw this movie about a shrink who wanted his client to confess something, so he stayed real quiet and stared the whole time, trying to make the guy nervous enough to spill the info. But Marie's not buying it.

"Is what true?" she asks again.

"I heard something about you."

She glances around the room, looking for the waiter. "And what did you hear, my dear?"

Don't "my dear" me. "Marie, I've been waiting almost three weeks to ask you something, something I'm dying to tell my mom, but you have to give me an extremely good reason why I shouldn't, because if I do, you're a goner."

She shifts nervously in her seat, eyes searching for our missing server. "Where the hell is this guy?"

Hell? Marie using the word *hell*? "Hello?" My mouth hangs open, and I shove my face into her line of view. "Did you hear me?"

"Yes. Yes, I heard you. What, Desert? What's the question?"

"Fine. Someone told me you hired that photographer. The one who came to our house last month."

She wipes her mouth with a napkin then smiles at our waiter, who hands her the check. While reviewing and signing the bill, she presses her lips together. Then she closes the case flap and looks directly at me. "Desert," she begins. "Let me explain something."

"That's why we're here."

She stares blankly, like she doesn't appreciate being interrupted or she doesn't recognize me. Then her eyes close and she breathes a long sigh. Finally she says, "I want you to know, not that you don't already, but just a reminder, that I love you. Very much."

Great. I want to believe this, but I'm not sure about anything right now. "Okay, so what's going on?"

She sighs heavily. When she reopens her eyes, I see they're glazed. "You're almost like my own daughter. I've watched you grow up, hon. I've seen you change. You've got lots of resentment."

"Resentment?"

"Toward your mom, honey."

"I don't have any resentment." Well, okay, maybe a little.

She grabs her purse. "Let's go. We'll talk on the way." Part of Marie's expertise is dealing with people who won't be happy with the news she might bring them, so I can tell she's using her skills on me now. Take the clients for a walk, so they won't make a scene in the restaurant.

"Let's talk here," I say, staying in my seat. Whatever she has to say, she can say it here.

"Honey, don't be silly. Let's go, come on." She nods toward the door, hurrying me along, like a toddler who doesn't want to budge.

"What resentment, Marie?"

She looks at me then sits back down. "Fine, you want to discuss this here?" she asks calmly, lowering her face, whispering. "Where people are actually listening, even though they're pretending not to? Where people who know exactly who you are are eavesdropping and you don't even know it?" She whips her head around to a man, sitting with a gray-haired woman at a table near us, and he immediately looks away. "Let's walk, shall we?"

How does she do that? Man, Marie's so in tune. "Fine."

We gather our things and leave the joint, strolling out into the blazing sun and tiled walkway. There are people everywhere, buying candles and sweet incense, sipping frozen drinks, listening to a local band. The atmosphere is definitely upbeat, but my heart feels like it's going to explode.

We walk past a boutique, where a stone bench awaits empty, and Marie takes a seat. I sit too. Like three feet from her.

"All right, baby, there's no easy way to say this, so I'll just come right out."

"Go ahead!" Before I rip it out of you!

She zips and unzips her purse, one of my mother's trademark quirks when she's nervous. "Crossfire's done, sweetie. They'll soon be history. They'd like to keep playing, but nobody's listening."

Well, nobody except Becca. "What does this have to do with the photographer?"

"Desert, don't you want to see them over and done with? Crossfire?"

"Well, sometimes, but—"

"I'm tired of seeing you angry, Desert! You were always such a happy little girl, and you've become so . . . disillusioned with everything. That kills me."

"I'm sixteen, Marie. Every sixteen-year-old is disillusioned with life."

"No. No, they're not. Not like you. Sweetie, if you were my daughter, I would've done things differently. I love your mom, and your dad," she says, looking down at her hands folded in her lap, "but I wouldn't have taken you on the road, hon. I think your folks made a huge mistake with that one."

So she agrees with me? "I don't get it."

"All I want is to see you happy, Des. I want to see you all settled down in one place, going to school, making friends, loving life, just like a girl your age should be doing, not tagging along with a bunch of burned-out musicians."

She's been listening. An adult who's actually been listening to me all along. But hey, easy on the burned-out part. My dad is still my dad. "So you're in this with Adriana? You hired the photographer for her article?"

For a moment she searches my face, worry spilling out of her, like any family member concerned over one of its troubled teens. Then she nods softly, eyes closing in admission.

"I don't believe this." I don't believe this!

"Desi," she says, reaching over to touch my knee. "I'm doing this for you, hon, you gotta believe me."

Strange. Weird. This would piss the hell out of my mom. But I believe it. Or do I just want to believe it? I don't know what to think. "So by getting this article printed, you think that'll be enough pressure to make Mom quit? But Mom doesn't care what's written about her anymore. Especially in some small-time tabloid."

"Usually. Unless it's about you, or her as a mother. If it attacks her as a parent, believe me, she's sensitive to it."

"This is too weird. I don't know what to say." To say the freakin' least.

"Isn't this what you want, Des? To see your parents settled

down, traveling occasionally, and yourself graduating from a school that you've actually attended a couple years straight without interruption? Think about it, Desi."

Think about it. Yes, let me do that, because I don't spend enough time as it is thinking about anything. We teens are so unmotivated, you know. This is everything I ever think about! It's what I confessed to Liam Friday night. It's only the whole reason I asked him to make up stories about me. To finally experience a normal childhood before my college ticket gets called and I'm on my own forevermore.

"Babalú?" I have to make sure I've got this straight.

"Desi?"

"You're betraying my parents . . . for me?"

She tilts her head and grimaces. "Betraying is a strong word, Des. Look, all the signs point to a breakup of the band anyway. I'm not the one controlling that. This would just be the straw breaking the camel's back."

You see? There's that stupid camel again.

"Don't tell your mother, Desert. She wouldn't understand. I've spent my whole career arguing about her choices regarding you. She's too stubborn."

I couldn't agree with her more, but still. For some reason, this doesn't add up. Why do it like this, in secret? Why not just talk to Mom and tell her how she feels? Why not just explain this to Dad? He'll listen!

"I know," I say. "But you do realize if they find out about this, you're out of a job."

"Of course, hon. It's all right. I've had offers lined up for years."

"Is that why you left for home?"

"No, I went for a break. Your folks asked me to. They needed one too, I think."

"Do you know why Mom's been down all week?"

Marie knows. She knows everything. She turns her face away, looking at something far off. "Probably the sessions. They're not working, Des, I'm telling you."

Yeah, she's right. They're sucking pretty bad. One song actually sounds like The Madmen on crack. "But I heard them. They would be okay if it weren't for Faith. She's the one who's throwing a wrench in their craft!"

Marie thinks this is funny and, I swear, I have never seen her look more guilty. "That's my girl."

Chapter Sixteen

Becca's quiet today. A little too quiet. Could she still be mad at Liam for not telling her that Flesh was moving to town the very second he found out? It's not like she didn't learn about it two days later anyway. But still, it's been a month since that happened—get over it already.

Becca wriggles her nose at the stench in the cafeteria. I swear schools should put comment cards on the tables so we can complain about how damn smelly it gets in here. I know that's what Brianna would do, for sure. This one time at St. Alf's, she made a huge fuss over the lunchroom stink, and they gave us all free dessert for three days.

"Reeks, right?" I ask, covering my nose with a napkin.

"The bathrooms," Liam says, popping open a juice carton.

"What about them?"

"That's what stinks. The guys' bathroom outside overflowed this morning. Nobody's fixed it yet, I guess."

"Gross," Becca mutters, eyes glued to her sheet music. She hasn't had a bite to eat. All she's done is finger invisible frets and pick at imaginary strings.

"It speaks!" I say, but Becca only smirks at me. Since my chat with Marie, I've wondered whether or not to finally tell Liam and Becca about the whole plan to foil Crossfire for my sake. I know my parents wouldn't appreciate it if I divulge insider info, especially when they don't know it themselves. But I really feel these guys are my friends.

Liam leans into my shoulder. "Desert, check out those guys down the table. Don't look right at them."

I pretend to search intensely for a maitre d' near the kitchen. I see what Liam's pointing out. These guys sitting there, sporting Crossfire—Insanity concert shirts, inching closer, like I'm gonna invite them to join us or something. "Can you believe that?"

"Yeah, that's pretty geeky." Liam laughs. "Come on, Desert, invite them over."

I shoot him a look. "No. Stop it."

He laughs again. "Right, Becca? We should have a great big Crossfire powwow right here at table eight?"

Becca grins, sighs, then finally pays attention to her tray of burritolike substance with cole slaw. It's unbelievable how anyone can eat this stuff. I go through the grueling task of preparing my own lunch each night just so I won't need to touch any of that garbage.

Halfway through my sandwich, someone behind me says, "Excuse me, Desert?"

I whirl around to find one of the guys with the Crossfire shirts. "Yeah? Hi?" He's coming to ask me for something, something related to the band probably. It's a greeting I recognize, full of hope that I'll get him something.

"I don't mean to bother you, but is there any way you can get your dad to sign these concert tickets?" he asks, showing me a pair of stubs from the last tour. "If not, it's cool. I just thought I'd ask."

See, this is a problem. If I say yes, then everyone will want something from me, and I just can't. I'm not Dad's agent or PR person. He's Dad, not Flesh. "Look, I'm sorry, I really am. I don't mean to be rude, but you understand that—"

"Oh, that's cool," the dude says, interrupting. "I know, you'd have to do it for everyone. That's cool. Sorry to bother you. Sorry." And he smiles, then goes back to the group of guys, who look disappointed.

I feel terrible. I really do. The guy was nice, but I just can't. It would get totally out of control. Liam and Becca stare at me, trying to empathize, trying to get used to this, their friend with all the odd attention. Thankfully, Becca decides this is a good time to change the subject by actually speaking.

"You guys, I've been talking to someone," she announces out of nowhere, looking down, as if she's talking to the guitar tabs.

I peer up into her face. "Someone as in a love prospect someone?"

"Who?" Liam asks, chowing down.

"This girl in my art class. I've known her since middle school, well, known her name. You might know her, Liam. Jessie?"

Liam acknowledges the name, but I can't tell what he's thinking.

"I guess she's always known me," she goes on. "But we never actually talked until last week."

"And?" Liam's swirling his juice carton in the air, urging for more info.

"And we paired up for an assignment, kinda the way you guys did in Ms. Smigla's class that time."

Liam elbows me. I smile like a goof.

"She's cool. We've been talking on the phone every night. I went to her house yesterday."

Liam's about to fall off the bench. "And? Did you get it on?"

"Liam!" she cries. "Cut it out! We just met, and I want to know what you guys think of her."

"Damn. All right, let's meet her then," Liam agrees.

"Yeah, awesome, Becca. Like when?"

"She's here." Becca's gaze darts around and lands somewhere across the room.

"Where?" I'm looking for someone who might be waving at us. Stupid thought.

"There. You see the blond girl in the green top, still in line?"

Let's see, there's a girl with her hair in cornrows, wearing a green, skintight piece of cloth, if that's what Becca's calling a top. "Yes?"

"That's Jessie."

I've seen her around. Sometimes she hangs out with Flute Girl, whose name I learned is Amber . . . gag. But usually I've seen Jessie in the Oye section of the parking lot. I guess she's part band friend, part Oye.

"*That* Jessie?" Liam looks like he's going to be sick.

"Why? What's wrong?" Becca asks, eyebrows drawn together.

"Nothing, I just can't believe you're seeing that girl," Liam says, but he doesn't offer an explanation for his grossed-out attitude. I'll have to squeeze what he knows out of him later.

"What makes her so nice?" I ask. I really must know, since this girl competes with the weirdness maximus crowd.

Becca sighs, shrugging. "I don't know. She just is. Knows a lot about music, I guess."

"Does she know about Desert here?" Liam asks.

I smack his arm. "Who cares?"

"She might. I haven't said anything, though." Becca glares at me, reminding me of the cold treatment I gave her the day my pictures were posted. I don't know what she's all sour about. I said I was sorry.

I did appreciate it, though. Her not going off and bragging like other kids usually have in the past. Jessie spots us and picks up speed. "She saw us, Beck. I think she's coming over."

Becca runs a hand through her straight hair, fluffing it up. I just noticed that she looks really nice today. She's got that eyeliner working again. Plus some lip gloss. So this is why she's been getting all dolled up lately. Go, Becca!

As Jessie gets closer I can see she's very hoochie-mama,

smacking her gum and everything. Hard to believe she knows much about anything other than body glitter, much less music. She walks up to our table and stands there, smiling.

"Hi!" Becca greets her. Beck looks different suddenly, like a happier, perkier version of herself.

"Hey, can I sit with you guys?" Hoochie asks, throwing her hip out.

What does Becca see in this chick?

"Sure," Liam says, scooting over toward me to make some room. He turns his head then whispers, joking, "Sorry, am I getting too close?"

Too close, my butt!

"Yeah, actually. Why don't you just sit on my lap?" I kid, pinching his bicep. He laughs. He totally gets me.

"Jessie, this is Liam and Desert," Becca says. Do I detect a flush on her cheeks, or is it just blush she's wearing too?

"Hi." Hooch gestures at Liam. "You, I know from P.G. Middle, but you, I don't think I ever met."

No, no, she's right about that. Because if I'd ever met her before, I sure as hell would remember those JLo jeans she's sportin' there. "No, don't think so, hi." I'm being really nice, considering she hasn't stopped staring at me since she parked her big butt down.

"Li's the one I was telling you about, Jessie. The one with the art collection," Becca says, but Jessie barely acknowledges her.

"Art collection?" I whisper. "You never told me you had an art collection."

"It's no big deal," Liam says shyly. "Just whatever I find I like, I print. My walls are covered with stuff."

"Ah, so you're a pirate?"

"A what?" Jessie asks, complete and total befuddlement all over her face. "Did she say 'a pirate'?"

"I meant, as in piracy, as in he's stealing images off the Internet." Can you say ignorant?

"No, I'm not," Liam defends himself. "I try to get the artist's permission to print it. Most of the time they reply."

I was just kidding anyway. "I didn't know you did that. That's cool." You know, I just realized that Liam and I haven't talked much about his hobbies. Everything's always about me. How totally self-centered.

We're there, listening to Jessie and Becca talk about some stupid Lifetime movie last night, when a loud-as-hell alarm screams out of nowhere. Fire drill. Some girls shriek as two hundred students make for the doors, laughing and hooting. Liam picks up our book bags. "Party!" he cries, pulling me to the nearest EXIT sign with him.

All these bodies trying to shuffle through this doorway like cattle make me want to moo. It also makes me want to wrap my arms around Liam, who's inching toward an exit. He wore a tight T-shirt today that accents a surprisingly athletic build underneath. Sexy and seventeen, baby, and he's all mine.

He reaches back and grabs my hand, pulling it around his waist. My, my. Then, he leans his head back and says, "This is perfect."

Yes, it is, isn't it? "What is?"

"This fire drill."

Oh.

"I've been wanting out of here all day. Can't concentrate on anything."

Wonder why. Could it be because of me? Does Liam think about me as much as I do about him? Ever since the cemetery last Friday, my thoughts have been all Liam, Mom, Marie, Liam, Becca, Marie, Liam, Liam, Adriana. Did I mention Liam?

"Hey, have you told your stepmom anything about me yet?" I ask. We enter the open corridor outside the cafeteria, and exit from the side of the building. Hopefully he knows where he's going. I'm just following his lead. Becca and Jessie got lost somewhere back there with the cattle.

"Yeah." He shrugs. No eye contact, all serious. "I tried. Said you're all friendly one minute and yelling at people the next."

"Geez, you don't have to make me sound schizophrenic."

"Whatever works." He laughs. "You mean, like Jessie?"

"Yeah? What is up with that girl? Why would Becca even like her? What could she possibly know about guitar, which is the only thing Becca even cares about? That and Flesh."

"That girl's a lunatic, man. She probably just buttered Becca all up about her art, and Becca flipped that someone was paying attention to her. I've heard she can be a real bitch."

"Becca?"

"No, you nerd! Jessie!"

We laugh like idiots. "Well, then maybe we should tell Becca something," I say.

"Nah. You can't tell her anything. She gets too sensitive. She's gotta figure things out on her own."

Very true. I can be like that too, I guess. "She wouldn't stop staring at me the whole time sitting there."

"Yeah, I know."

So he noticed too. I don't want to be the one to tell Becca, but I recognize this weird feeling as butt kissing. The story of my life. I'm the stepping-stone people walk over to reach Flesh. "Whatever. She seems happy. Let her have fun, I guess."

Liam tows me to the parking lot, where hundreds of kids are lined up outside the fence. A few smoking, most chatting. Fire drills are like the ultimate excuse to socialize on campus. Me, I'm getting escorted to a nice red Integra, which Liam clicks open with the remote on his keychain.

"This your brother's?" I ask, sliding my hand along the smooth, waxed body.

"Yes, ma'am," he says, opening the car door for me, showing me in. "Hope he doesn't need it in the next five minutes."

Two seconds later, a taller, chubbier version of Liam is standing next to us. "I see we both had the same idea," says the stranger.

"Hey, Mike." Liam bumps shoulders with him. "You mind if I hang out here for a bit?" He sends Michael the universal, guy-to-guy, *I've-got-a-chick-with-me-now-scram* look.

"No, man, that's fine. Is this Desert?" he asks, smiling and nodding at me.

Is this Desert? So I guess Liam talks about me. Or maybe Adriana talks about me. Does Michael think I'm Liam's girlfriend or a reconnaissance project?

"Yeah, Des, this is Michael," he says to me, then turns to his brother, "who's just about to leave."

"Nice to meet you," I say. I always feel archaic whenever I say that.

Michael says, "All right, all right, I'm outta here." He laughs and leaves to hang out with some friends along the fence. I get into the car, and Liam closes the door.

You know, I don't think I've ever been inside a vehicle that didn't belong to anyone in Crossfire, wasn't rented, or owned by a city guide. And Dylan, my boyfriend in LA, didn't have his license yet. This car's pretty nice, complete with leather everything.

Liam walks around the front, then opens the driver's side and gets in. He starts the ignition, cranks up the air, then leans his seat back. "Ahh! Awesome! Let's hang out till the all-clear bell rings."

"Let's stay," I suggest with a wicked smile.

He smiles back. Thank God. Houston, we have confirmation of mutual makeout.

I tilt my seat back to the same level as his, turning sideways to face him. "So, where'd you get those eyes?" I swear they're like gemstones.

"Last I knew, I was born with them."

"No, you dork! I mean, who has blue eyes in your family? Aren't you Spanish?"

"So?" He shrugs. "Lots of Hispanics have blue and green eyes. Hispanic means 'from Spain,' which is in Europe, you know. Europeans look like anything."

Blah, blah. Blah, blah, blue eyes, blah. "Come here, you," I say, leaning into the center console just as Liam moves in too. Our lips meet, soft and warm. After a little while, our hands begin to roam. Over necks, arms, waists, thighs. Nothing serious, but this is how it starts.

This is heaven. Really, truly, right here. In this car. Kissing Liam Blanco. Finally I feel like Desert, not Flesh's kid, not anybody other than plain ol' Des. Here with Li.

And a thought suddenly hits me. If Marie's plan doesn't work, if Crossfire goes on to make the new album, we'll be gone again, uprooted. On the road. Crazy, screaming fans. Bus aisles for beds. Planes. Sleeping across time zones.

And that means only one painful thing to me right now. No Miami, no Liam.

We stay in the car well into fifth period. I'll just tell Madame Girard tomorrow that I wasn't skipping, I was practicing my French out in the field. During sixth period I can't process a single word Mr. Evans says. Too many things on my mind. Too many to count. Only my pen tries to make sense of things.

Go, if you wish
But leave me here
I don't want to roam.
Moonlit park
Kiss the dark
Blue eyes home.

Chapter Seventeen

Obviously J. C. didn't get it when I said Becca plays guitar. I didn't mean a Fender. Now he's showing her all the essentials for setting up a multitrack, digital recording suite. From converters to recording/editing software, everything you'd need for laying down the basic tracks to polishing the final mix.

Becca's completely speechless but happy. Her eyes are packing years' worth of awe of a place only dreamed about in her little bedroom.

J. C. drapes a guitar over his chest. "See, what you wanna do is pedal the open A, like this." *Waaaang.* "Then you palm mute the power chords, like this." *Wa-oh, wa-oh.* "Then you alternate the picking for the sixteenth notes." *We-eee!* "And if you wanna get these pings, you gotta choke up on the pick."

Pedal, power, palm, picking, ping, pick. Dr. Seuss could've had fun with those.

"There's music out there, Rebecca, music beyond top forty," J. C. says, pushing his black hair behind his ears, grabbing his glass full of clinkiness. "You just gotta find it."

Okay, maybe it's time for J. C. to continue finding transcendental nirvana or higher vodka or whatever the hell he was seeking when we came in, before he scares Becca away.

"Girlies." Dad rushes in with that get-ready-to-work attitude. "Time to go. Out of the booth, come on. Wait outside if you want."

Phil, in his usual way of communicating without words, hands me his bass with a smile, pretend-suggesting that I play the parts instead of him.

I take his cue. "Dad! You mean you don't want us in here? Come on, look, I can do it. No melody outshining, just keep rhythm, right, Phil?"

Phil pulls back his precious instrument, wiping the strings down with a cloth, all with that silent grin of his.

"Very funny. Out!" Dad smacks my butt with his iBook. To Becca, he simply grins. He's probably not thrilled that she's here, but that's just too bad. She's staying. I need her.

"Don't we get to watch?" Becca asks me, all worried.

"Through here," I say, showing her the door to the waiting room. "Hey, so where's Jessie today? Are you guys still talking?"

"Yeah, we are, but not today. What did you guys think of her?"

Skanky. "She's nice."

Becca plops down on the sofa and raises an eyebrow. "Yeah, sure. Liam didn't look thrilled yesterday. I don't care."

"And is she interested in you? Like, you know. . . ?"

She brings her thumb to her lips and nibbles off a piece of skin. "I think so. She's said she's into both guys and girls."

"She did? She actually said that? How do you come around to things like that in conversation?" How do you find out from someone if they're gay, too? That must be so weird.

"I guess she picked up a vibe. Probably saw it in my eyes or something."

"Well, that's good eye-reading, right?" I ask, reaching over to grab a bag of Chex mix on the snack table. I pull it open.

"Yeah, the only problem is, she keeps talking about you and asking questions."

See? I knew it. Not good. "Like what?" I ask, picking out the pretzel pieces from my handful of mix.

"Like if I've been to your house, and if I've met your dad, and what he's like, and all that."

Great. A leech. Becca hooked a leech. And she doesn't see this? Maybe she sees it but doesn't care.

"I don't care, though," she admits, grabbing some snack mix. "She's nice to me."

Look what the cat dragged in. Enter Faith, towing a bag full of beach crap, hair thrown back into a knot, no makeup. She sees us and does a great impression of someone who could care less. "Coffee," she mutters.

"Over there." I point to the little table in the corner, complete with mugs, filters, creamers, and an assortment of sweeteners.

She'll be insulting me in three . . . two . . . "What do you care . . . Beach . . . Sand, I mean Desert?" Faith growls, glancing at me out of the corner of her eye.

How totally original. She should write pop songs! Someone overdosed on tanning oil this morning.

"Just being nice," I say with a grin.

"Why?" She throws her bag into the corner.

"No reason."

Because ultimately, you'll get me a permanent home. I've gotta be nice to you, Freak.

Instead I say, "I've realized how important it is having you around. Your input is really going to boost this ticket to where it needs to go, Faith."

Becca squeezes my arm, whispering, "Adams?"

"Shh," I respond, still smiling at the tanned demon before me.

Faith freezes, except for her tongue clicking. I'd say she's scared, half expecting to see the aliens who've abducted the regular Desert and replaced her with this ray of sunshine, pop out of the utility closet.

"What are you on?" she asks with a sneer.

"I'm not on anything. Meet my friend Becca."

Remember when you took your first-grade pictures and the photographer said, "Say cheese," and you'd just widened your mouth, showing teeth, but not smiling the least bit? This is the greeting Faith bestows on Becca before asking, "Is this the girl you said you couldn't be friends with?"

I love Faith. She's such a doll. Maybe if I glare at her hard enough I can burn a hole into her forehead.

"What is she talking about?" Becca asks, all innocent, watching Faith disappear into the corner café.

"The first day of school, when I saw your notebook, the one that says 'Flesh is a god.'"

Becca examines her lap. "Oh, that one."

"I just wasn't sure at first we could become friends, but look—look where you ended up." I gesture to the lovely interior of South Beach Sounds, surely a dream come true for Becca.

"True." She sighs sadly. *Is there any pleasing this girl?* "I can't believe that's Faith Adams. Isn't it weird how things turn out sometimes?" she asks, hugging a sofa cushion like it's a floatation device and she's drowning.

Yeah, like how Becca happens to be Dad's biggest fan, my boyfriend is the stepson of an evil tabloid reporter, and my mother's best friend is setting up the family business for failure. Sounds like something out of a movie.

A voice crackles on the speaker. "Adams, we need you in here." Max and Phil trample into the sound booth just as Dad's making his announcement.

"Coffee, I'm getting coffee, you prune," Faith replies, fully knowing my dad can't hear her. She flings the stirring stick onto the floor. My first urge is to run over there and yank her bleached hair right out of her scalp. But then I think about home, staying in Miami, being with Liam, and suppressing that rage gets easier.

"Did she just say. . . ?" Becca starts, but I nudge her.

"Yes, a joy, isn't she?" I try picturing Marie on the phone with Faith, convincing her to join the recording efforts. What could she have told her? *Hey, if you record with Crossfire, you'll help them down that spiral path?*

"I can't believe I'm here," Becca says. "This is so totally awesome!" Her knee begins to bob up and down.

Look at her, all google eyed, like a kid in a candy store. "Get over it."

She doesn't even hear me, because the session begins with a blast. Literally. Someone's blown a speaker or a monitor, and I can see Dad, Ryan, and the engineers are extremely thrilled about this. After some replacements and fine tuning, they start again with a song they've been calling "Number Two." It's been a couple of weeks since I gave them a big listen, and I have to admit, they're sounding a lot tighter. But that's without Faith's lyrics. Looks like Dad's stalling on that.

Mom just walked in. Her face is all pale. Marie's two paces behind, as usual, but they're not, like, together. Marie glances over, gives me a sympathetic grin, and sits at the desk with the laptop. Mom leans against the wall and lights up. This is the most I've ever seen her smoke.

After laying down some basic tracks, all but Dad and Faith leave the sound booth. Vocals. This is just what Becca's been waiting for, but I haven't exactly told her there's no reason to get her hopes up, considering Faith's been working on them. They start with a song appropriately called "Number Four." Dad lets loose his trademark falsetto, the one that begins half his songs, only this one's a ballad. And then, ladies and gentlemen, the horror . . .

"Baby, I miss you . . . lying here in my room . . . cannot forget you . . . woohoohoo," sings Flesh, only it can't possibly be Flesh. Apparently the same aliens that abducted and replaced the real Desert McGraw have caught hold of her father, too.

But Becca is forgiving and dedicated. She remains calm, listening. She adores Flesh, like her notebook says, and she knows there must be better stuff coming shortly, right?

"I love you so much, baby . . . aching for you, yeah, aching for you," Faith adds, doing her best to sound like a singer, all the while sliding her hand up my dad's arm.

Against the wall Mom scoffs, grinding out a stub on the adjoining glass, then leaves. A waning smile straightens Becca's lips. Halfway through the next putrid number she gives up, leaning back into the sofa, saddened by the unforgivable passing of Flesh.

Staring straight ahead, she asks, "What the hell is this?"

I never realized how echoey this room can be, listening to my laughter multiplied over and over again. If I wasn't so sure it was me, it could sound like some mad scientist cackling at his success in reanimating dead tissue. Catching my breath, I wheeze, "This is a sad, sad ending for Crossfire!"

Marie was right. They are self-destructing anyway. Those have got to be the worst, pop-sounding, bubble-gum-chewing, teeny-bopper crap lyrics I have ever heard.

Awesome.

Chapter Eighteen

It's been a week since Becca's disillusionment at the studio. She's still trying to get over it by listening and relistening to our whole discography. I'm at my locker, getting my copy of a rare import Crossfire CD she wanted to borrow, when some guy appears next to me.

"Hey, you Desert McGraw?" he asks.

"Yeah."

"Dude, your dad's band used to be really hot, like when my grandfather was in elementary school."

No, wait. Is he serious? Is he seriously standing here, insulting me to my face, thinking I haven't got any feelings whatsoever? "Really?"

"Yeah, man."

"Then that would make him the youngest twelve-year-old to ever have children to bear a scummy little punk like you."

He stands there, biting his lower lip. Five feet away his slightly smarter buddy chides, "Bro, you asked for it."

What a great way to start the day. I walk away without another word.

Liam waits for me outside Smig's class every day now that Becca hangs out with Hoochie most of the time, making me walk alone to class. He leans on the wall, leg bent at the knee, looking very James Dean.

"What happened, babe?" *Babe*, that's new. "Bad hair day?" He thinks he's being funny. Great, just the kind of support I was hoping for.

I head past him to the classroom. He pulls my arm back. "Sorry, Des. You okay?"

"Fine. Just some jerks getting on my back about my dad."

"Who?" Liam glances down the hallway, searching.

"I don't know who. Remember, I'm new here." Why, does he want to beat them up for me? That'd be kind of chivalrous and cool if he'd do that. "Just some idiots after homeroom. Don't worry about it."

"Well, I worry."

"Don't."

"Can't help it."

"Why?" I've been wondering this for a while now. "Why do you care so much about me, Liam?"

"What do you mean?"

Let's see, what do I mean? "I mean, why do you care so much about me?"

He looks around, turning up his palm. "You wanna talk about this now? The bell's gonna ring."

"Yeah, that stupid bell always telling us what to do. You're right. Forget it."

"No, wait. Okay," he begins, trying to think up a response to this impromptu question. "The first day I saw you, when you came in, and Smigla called your name, you looked like a deer caught in the headlights. Then you got defensive and shot everyone a dirty look. At first I thought you were just in a bad mood, but then I found out who you really were, and I felt bad for you, that you had to do that. That must suck."

"So that's it? That's why you're with me? Because you feel sorry for me?"

"That's not what I—" He reaches for my face.

I push his hand away. "Well, I don't need your pity. Give me any other excuse. Tell me you think I'm nice, have a sweet ass, anything, I don't care, but don't tell me you feel sorry for me."

"Jesus, all I meant was . . ."

"Honestly, I thought you'd say because I make you laugh, or you think I'm smart, or I'm likable."

"Likable?" He snorts. "You make that difficult." He turns on his heels and enters the classroom.

Nice. Thanks, Liam. Thanks. So now I'm not likable.

Becca rushes up. "Everything okay?"

"No, everything's not okay." I shove the CD into her hands. "Liam's mad at me."

Becca's become immune to my ranting. She leans in, hand resting on my shoulder. "Why? What happened?" Finally some genuine concern.

"Nothing. He thinks I'm unlikable."

"No!" Her hand flies up to her mouth. She's also picked up the art of sarcasm from somewhere.

"All right, just forget you all," I say, starting into class. If this is how my friends are gonna treat me . . .

"Desert, look, Liam had a bad night last night, okay? Did you even ask him about it?"

No. Not really. The thought didn't even cross my mind. Pausing at the door, I shake my head. "That doesn't give him an excuse to—"

Becca cuts me off. "You're incredible, you know that? His dad started a drinking binge a few days ago that ended with him acting like king of the goddamn universe last night, cursing, screaming at everybody, breaking things. And you know Liam, he watched it all happen without a word. So he's no doubt looking forward to seeing you, and all you give him is crap?"

Who is she, all high-and-mighty Protector of the Brotherhood? What the hell? You know, who needs this garbage? But then, I remember.

I do. *I* need this garbage.

I need Liam, and I need Adriana, and I better go apologize. Not just because of the article, but hell, because Liam's a great guy. Fine, I've been stupid.

Ms. Smigla's talking to a student, a quiet argument about a missing homework assignment. She could easily take all morning convincing the kid of the relevance of cinquains to our lives. I take advantage at Liam's desk.

"Hey, sorry," I say stupidly.

He jiggles his pen, the point making little dots in one spot on his paper. "It's all right." Without looking up.

"Liam?" I wait for his eyes to meet mine. "I'm sorry. Seriously. I didn't know you had a bad night. I'm sorry I didn't even ask."

"You know, you didn't even let me finish."

"Sorry!" How many times does he want me to say it?

"What I was going to say out there was the fact that the words you wrote that day—pleading, crying, trying to connect, those—they struck me."

They struck him? Okay. "Why? They were just about fans at a concert."

His eyes scan my face. Those eyes with the ability to make my stomach leap. "Were they?"

I think about this. For about two seconds. "Okay, Dr. Freud, whatever. Liam, don't read into it. They were just words." Yeah, okay. I don't ever write just words. I always choose them carefully. Always.

"If you say so. Regardless of what you think they meant, they made me feel something . . . for you. That power came to you easily."

"Power?" Has he been talking to J. C. and the New Age fairies who follow him around?

"Yes, that was the whole point of the assignment, remember? To create a powerful message? You did it easily, and what's more, you even did it so that we each took different meanings from it. That's good writing. I liked that about you."

Oh.

"Is that a good enough reason?"

I guess so. I nod, smiling. "Thanks, Liam."

"And something else," he says.

"What?"

"You have a sweet ass."

After school Liam and I kiss, deep and long. I'm really glad we didn't get into a full-blown fight. When he finally leaves, he winks my way as his brother pulls out of the parking lot. Me, I really don't feel like going home today. There's some weird vibes going on over there with my dad, Mom, Marie, and everything. I don't really want to be a part of it.

So I hang out by the front of the school, near the bus stop. Underneath a big ficus tree I sit. People I don't even know walk by saying hi to me, waving politely, hoping I'll say hi, then trying to control their enthusiasm if I do. I feel famous, even though I'm not. I'm not! I haven't done anything special, ever!

Suddenly Jessie, the hoochie-mama, is next to me, taking the liberty to sit for a little chat, like she's known me her whole life.

"Desert, what's up?"

Definitely not that hair. Or those chains. "Hey, Jessie." I almost called her Hooch for a second there.

"Who you waiting for?" She smacks her gum.

"Nobody in particular. Becca left already?"

"What? Oh, Becca. Yeah, said she had to go home. Probably to play guitar. Weird, right?"

"No. Why would that be weird?" Good, I'm glad I said it.

"I dunno. All that guitar playing she does, like she's gonna make it big or famous or something like that, right?"

Again, no. Let's cut to the chase. "Can I help you with something?"

She smiles, then slides her tongue across her lower lip. Gross. "Oye . . ."

And you thought I was stereotyping.

"Listen, is there any way possible, you know, that maybe some of my friends and me, we could, I dunno, meet your dad in person?"

Isn't this lovely.

"Why?" I ask.

Her eyebrows shoot up. "Why?"

"Yes, why? It's a legitimate question, no?"

Her face suggests I'm in need of some serious adjustments. "Because your dad's Flesh, right?"

Oh, my God! She's right! I should have known that!

"Look. Jessie. I don't really bring people home to meet my dad. He doesn't like it. He's actually very . . . shy."

"Really?" Her head tilts, totally not what she was expecting.

"Yeah. People think he's all cool, you know rock 'n' roll and beat the system man, all that crap, but he's really into bubble baths."

"'Scuse me?" Any sexual attraction she had for the guy is now busted. Good, one less person he needs yearning for him.

"I know. It's shocking."

She stares at me, through me. Anyone home?

"And cats," I add.

"Cats?"

"I know. Please don't tell anyone, okay? It would be so humiliating if everyone found out."

Please tell everyone. Everyone you meet, so they'll leave me the hell alone.

I wander the Grove for a while before going home. Finally, around four, I slip the key into the door, amble to our great room, and find my dad—my workaholic dad who stops at nothing, sitting on the couch, fighting tears.

Chapter Nineteen

I've never seen him on the verge like this. On the verge of being pissed, yes. On the verge of losing patience, sure. But not on the verge of tears.

"Dad? What happened?"

Silence. Biting of his lip, squeezing a couch pillow. He shakes his head like he wants to tell me, like he needs someone to listen, but he can't. He just can't. I'm not the right person.

But I want him to talk to me. I mean, I know I'm not Ryan or Marie, but he can, if he'll just give me a chance. This isn't like him, and honestly, it's freaking me out. My dad is the rock in this family. The stable one. If he loses it, who do I have to hold on to?

"Want a Coke?" I ask. If he agrees to one, then maybe he wants me around.

He nods. Good.

I walk into the kitchen and notice a glass in the sink. Broken. And next to it on the counter, a plate. Smashed. My stomach rolls. Something happened. Did Marie tell them something? Did she give up and come clean? At this point, it's either that or the band folded.

"Careful in the kitchen," Dad says, his voice weak and tired. He hadn't spoken yet. Until now, to warn me. Funny, no matter what's going on, my dad finds his sanity long enough to make sure I stay out of danger. "Don't cut yourself."

I open the fridge and pull out two cans of soda. One with lemon, for Dad. I return to the great room, noticing the cobwebs in the vaulted corner of the ceiling. And a box, still unopened from the move, next to the entertainment center. Maybe it's time we hired help around here. It's been two months already. I hand Dad the can, then sit on the couch.

He doesn't ask me to leave. Instead he pulls in his feet to sit cross-legged on the couch. He shoves a cushion into the open space and leans into it. Then he reaches over and sets the soda can, still unopened, down on the coffee table. His fingers begin pulling lint off the cushion.

"Girly," he says, clearing his throat.

"Yeah, Dad?"

"I don't know if you realize"—he pauses, gathering his words—"but things have been a little tense around here."

"Tense?" I fake innocence, tilting my head like a puppy hearing a high-pitched whistle.

He sighs. Maybe I should be trying to make this easier, not harder on him.

"Okay," I say. "I've noticed a little. Are you all right? Is it the recording? How's that coming along?"

"It's not working, Desert. Well, maybe I shouldn't say that. Some things are working, but some aren't. We made a mistake by bringing in new personnel." His thumb and forefinger massage the muscles beneath his eyebrows, the surefire sign of my dad under stress.

New personnel. Faith, he means.

"Bad business move," he goes on. "But it's not just that. That's fixable."

Fixable. Okay, so what's not fixable? I say nothing, knowing my dad needs no prompting. If he wants to speak, he will.

His head drops into his hands. His body shudders. This is bad. Whatever it is. And you know what? I don't care what's going on. Whatever it is, we'll do something about it. We can get through this. All I know is this is killing him—and me.

Just please, God, don't let it be cancer or death or something. Oh, God, I just thought of that. No, please! My hands start shaking.

I set my drink on the coffee table, leap over to him, and wrap my arms around his neck. My head on his shoulder. Immediately I feel his body leaning into me, needing me, drawing strength. I've never seen him like this. He seems so . . . frail.

I can't take this. My face swells, and suddenly I'm crying too, realizing how amazing human beings are, that empathy can manifest itself physically. Like a pregnant woman's husband, feeling pains and discomfort on her behalf. I can feel my dad's pain.

"Girly," he says again, sobbing.

Suddenly I'm all too aware that he was alone in the house when I came home. No Faith prancing around. No Marie on the phone. No Mom. "Dad?" A cruel image of an ambulance, a car smashed, a stretcher, and spattered blood flashes through my head, and I find myself sweating. "Where's Mom?"

He sobs some more.

"Dad? Stop it, you're scaring me!" I shout.

At this he stops and looks up, expression mixed of guilt and surprise. "Oh, honey, I'm so sorry. She's fine. She's fine. I didn't mean to scare you."

Jesus! Thank you!

"She's just gone." He waves his palm, like he's lost control of the situation.

"Where?" I ask, feeling my stomach contract.

"I don't know. She left, didn't say where she was going. She's upset."

"Upset at what?" It *was* Marie! Marie admitted the truth. But why would she? So early in the game? The band's not even split yet. Or are they?

"At me," he says into the cushion, then looks directly into my eyes. "At me."

At him? But I don't get it. "Dad?" I question, searching his face, because he's managed to create a wide range of emotions within me, without telling me what the hell's happening.

"Girly, your mother's mad because I haven't exactly been

146

telling her the truth. I've been keeping something from her, something that's been eating away at me. Something"—he pauses—"I did."

"And that would be?" I ask, accusing. This is not sounding good. Not good at all.

"Jesus," he blurts, forcing a weak smile at me. "I didn't think of how the second woman I love more than anything would take this." He exhales deeply, shaking his head again.

"Take what, Dad? How should I even know how I'm supposed to take something, if you won't even tell me what it is?"

Eyes down, he says, "I've cheated on your mother, Des."

"What?"

Cheated on your mother. Cheated. Great. This is just super. Suddenly the voices of hundreds of people over the years—interviewers, disc jockeys, schoolmates, friends, enemies—talking about my father, his image, the rock star, the glamour, the women, the sex, the private rooms, the abundance of it all, whoosh into my mind. I never wanted to believe it. Any of it. I just didn't see it. He's always been so strong, so resilient, so perfect. So perfect.

"But you love Mom!" I yell. "Don't you? This doesn't make sense! With who, Dad?"

Why is he doing this? My stomach squeezes tighter.

"Doesn't matter. It's between me and your mom. I only wanted you to know, so you wouldn't be left in the dark. Especially now that she's gone."

My mother can't be gone. She wouldn't leave me! Why does he keep saying that?

"I can't believe this. How could you do this? Why? Why, Dad?"

Stupid question. Why? Because his life has been half-spent surrounded by beautiful women, young women, girls only slightly older than me, women eager and willing to do anything he wants, no strings attached. Every man's fantasy. A bevy of Venusian angels falling at his feet. And he's a man, right? No man could resist that . . . right?

I don't know. My dad's not just any man.

"Desert, it was a mistake. It hasn't been going on for a long time. Whatever anybody out there may tell you, whatever you may hear. I do love your mom, Des. I've always loved her." He pauses, taking my hands, kneading. "This doesn't change that. I know that sounds absurd. We don't want to hurt the ones we love, but sometimes it just happens."

It just happens. Yeah, sure, okay. I jerk my hands out of his.

"No, you know what? It doesn't just happen!" I bark, mostly because I can't think of anything else. This is a shock, to say the freakin' least. He may be a man, but I think he's also completely capable of a little self-control. He's not a sheep or a monkey, for Christ's sake. I don't care who he is! "You hurt Mom," I shout, finger pointing then turning it right around, "you hurt me!" I take off toward the stairs. There's really nothing left to say.

"Desert," he calls pitifully. No doubt he feels like shit. Not sure if that's a good thing. I mean, I do love him.

A thought crosses my mind, standing there, hand clutching the railing. I turn around and ask, "What's gonna happen? Are you and Mom gonna split up? 'Cause you know what? That'd be just great! Then my life really would be just like everyone else's! Another child of divorced parents. Hey, I'd be in the majority!"

"I don't know what's going to happen," he says, lowering his head again. "First I need her to come home, so we can talk about it."

This is just fantastic. All I need. Here I thought the only real thing going for me was the fact that my parents were still together, still going strong, while all around me everyone else's parents were going separate ways. Here I've been, all these years, defending him against the skeptics, those who just love to rub it in my face that my dad was fallible, that he had to be, because of his very profession. And I'd defended him. I'd defended him!

I guess Becca was right. He was godlike. Even in my eyes.

I guess we were wrong.

Chapter Twenty

chasms widen, mountains quake
Rumbling stones upturn
Boulders crash to the valley below
waters churn, fires burn
comets gaining steadily
On a fatal path
To blast this rock straight into hell
we suffer unending wrath

From: saharagobi@crossfire.com

To: "Brianna Roman"

Subject: you suck

i have no freakin' clue why I'm still writing to u. did u see marie when she went to visit? did she tell you anything interesting? do u even know what's going on over here? do you care? are you even alive? forget u

D

Chapter Twenty-One

I *called Liam last* night after the wonderful news about my father's infidelity. He listened, for a good three hours, to my theories about men. "Sex. That's what it's ultimately about, isn't it?" I had asked.

"Not necessarily," he had replied. "Don't simplify us like that."

But when I enter Liam's weekend room, the one at his dad's house, there's artwork highlighting the female form everywhere. Nothing tasteless. Not to me, anyway. Just shapes, silhouettes, copies of work, created in oil, pastels, mosaic tiles, pencil, computer-generated drawings, photos. Everything framed and matted.

"Yes, I can see how you didn't want me simplifying your existence here on earth," I say, eyeing a charcoal drawing of a woman's bare back, hair swept up, the nape of her neck, beautiful.

"Well, you said it like men are dogs, like, all they care about is sex. And that's not always true. I'm sure some guys are like that, but not all of them."

He must be joking.

"Liam, puh-leez. This isn't news to the world. It may be hard for you to hear, because it sounds so inhuman, but it's the truth, and nothing could be more human. It's always about sex. Why deny it? Don't worry, I understand."

But Liam looks wounded. "You insult me, Desert. You insult me." Palm at his chest, mock shock.

But I got him. I know I did. He's just doing the politically correct guy thing to do. Denying it.

"Wanna hear why I'm right?" I ask. I love this.

"Please enlighten me, O Informed One," he says, rolling his eyes.

I shoot him a hard stare. "Okay, it's basic biology. Tell me, when are men fertile?"

"What?" Liam retracts, looking like he'd rather be anywhere than here at this point.

"Just answer me."

"I don't know! Whenever?"

"Exactly. Whenever. Men are biologically designed to be fertile at any point at any given time. Day or night. Rain or shine. That's why they're always horny."

"Damn!" Liam says, looking anywhere but at me.

"Am I right?"

He's completely humiliated, I can see. His ears are pink. "Fine," he admits.

"Because it's their biological role, to be ready to go forth and multiply at all times. It's not their fault. That's just how they're programmed. And women are horny, when?"

"Never. Unless you're watching porn, then it's always."

"Very funny, jerk."

Liam smiles.

"Marie says that women are horny when they're ovulating. That's once, once a month," I explain.

"That sucks." Liam sulks.

"Why? That's just nature controlling things, so we humans don't get overpopulated."

"And why are we having this conversation?" he asks, raising his eyebrows.

"Because you think men are beyond sex, but they're not. It's on their minds, twenty-four seven. That's how nature intended it. The thought is always there. You only learn to control it."

He's thinking about this. I can see he needs some encouragement.

"Okay, look, men aren't like dogs, you say? Well, I'll prove you wrong."

"This should be interesting."

I'll ignore that. "Men are so much like dogs, they can be trained," I challenge.

"Whatever you say."

"Take your dad. Is he married?"

"Yeah, so's yours."

"Right. There, they've been trained. Because no guy in his right mind would ever get married if he fully realized the gravity of the situation. But the promise of sex makes him do it. He figures he'll always have someone around to screw when he feels like it. And that seals the deal. Boom, next thing you know, he's walking down the aisle."

"That's a load of crap."

"Is it?"

"Yes," he says flatly. "Maybe he wants companionship. Maybe he wants kids."

"Ah, see? Sex again. Can't have kids without sex."

"What are you getting at?" he asks, taking a seat at his computer desk.

And I realize . . . I have no clue. Only that everything I've ever believed about men was formed by the way I felt about Dad. And now that's changed. Now I don't know what to think. "I don't know. I'm just trying to sort all of this out."

"Let me ask you something," Liam says, picking up a tennis ball and bouncing it back and forth against the door. "If that's the case, what you're saying, then explain your dad."

"Leave him out of this." He is *not* going there.

"No, wait, seriously. If that's the case, then why'd your dad get married? Here's this guy who can get laid any night of the week, by the most gorgeous of women."

"Stop it."

"Sorry, I'm not trying to remind you. But if what you're saying is true, then it wouldn't make any sense for your dad to have gotten married. If sex would have come easier to him by staying single, then why get married?"

"Because of love, you dingbat." Dad loves Mom. That much I know. That's why this doesn't make sense. That's why it hurts so damn much.

"You see? Who's the dingbat now, baby? Who's the dingbat? Who's the dingbat?" His arms do a victory dance.

How'd he do that? I don't like my theories getting disproved.

"And don't think for a second that women can't be trained too," he adds with a hint of challenge.

Ah, so he agrees with me? But he's wrong. "Liam, you can't train a woman any more than you can train a cat."

At this he leans over laughing, and I thank God for Liam's sense of humor, or else we could be at this Mars-Venus crap all night.

Quiet for a while, Liam surfs the Net while I peruse his art collection. Breasts, butts, bellies, all smooth bodies, all perfect, even the pictures of the not-so-skinny women. At least he has those up too. That's a first. A memory of Dylan nags me. Of him ragging on some of the girls at school, the ones anyone anywhere would consider to be normal, but at St. Alf they were seen as fat. But Liam has them on his wall. Art to be seen. And appreciated.

"So when does she get home?" I ask. Funny, even the thought of meeting the woman who could ruin my mom's reputation hasn't made me forget my parents' dilemma.

"Adri? She should be home soon." He leans back to stretch. When he does this, his shirt pulls up, revealing nice, cut abs. Jock abs. Liam could play any sport if he wanted to, just because of those abs. But he doesn't. What does he do? He collects art.

And I'm staring at him, why? "Did you tell her I was coming?" "Nope."

Great. Surprise visit from Matti McGraw's daughter. She'll probably think I came to kick her butt.

"Listen, she'll probably ask you questions. You don't have to answer any of it if you don't want."

"Thanks, Liam, I know that."

"Believe it or not, Des, Adriana feels bad for your situation. She's on your side, I think."

I'm not even sure what side I'm on anymore. What used to be clear sides are now starting to blur together. Are Marie and Adriana really on my side? Why would Marie betray my parents, even if it was for me? Does that mean she loves me more than she loves them? And now Adriana is on my side, says Liam.

"Liam, your stepmom's a journalist. She's got her own agenda. She doesn't care about me. She doesn't even know me."

"She doesn't have to know you to sympathize. And you're wrong. She doesn't have her own agenda. She just feels strongly about parenting. Freedom of speech, baby."

Sympathize. Is it really that bad? Maybe tag-along touring isn't so bad. What am I saying? Of course it is. God, I feel I don't know anything anymore. My brain is a ball of mush. Thoughts of

Liam and mush. I rub my eyes.

"What's wrong?"

"Nothing. Didn't get much sleep last night."

A door closes at the opposite end of the house. The jingle of keys. Something being set down. Bags of groceries maybe. Voices of little kids, squealing.

"There. She's home. Let's go," Liam says, jumping up. Has he been waiting for this?

We trek through the hallway. Photos engulf us from both sides. Little Liam, sandy blond, cutie smile, missing teeth. Carrie, maybe? Doing a handstand. His brother, Michael, more menacing, with Liam in a headlock. Two younger girls with dark eyes, his half sisters. A nineties-dressed dad. A wedding picture. Dad and a dark-haired, thin woman. Adriana.

Suddenly it all seems a little too surreal. What would Mom say if she knew I was here? It'd go something like this: *It's time to kill you, Desert. And really give the dirt-diggers something to write about.* But have I sided with the enemy? No, I'm just visiting the enemy's lair. How different can Mom and Adriana really be, though? I mean, aren't they both mothers, doing what they feel is right for their children? Don't they share this much in common, at least?

In the kitchen the same woman from the wedding picture stands at the refrigerator door, rearranging its contents to make room for new items. Only she's older, more worn, little lines around her eyes.

"Adri," Liam says, startling her out of her skin.

She drops a ketchup bottle but catches it against her body before it hits the floor. "*Ay, mi hijito!* I didn't know you were here. Weren't you going to the movies with Michael?"

Liam presses his lips, looks at me. "I was. Something else came up."

Me. I came up. Didn't know he had plans already. I guess I should've asked first before inviting myself over.

"Oh, hi!" Adriana says, realizing he has company. Her smile is bright, brown eyes to match.

"Um," Liam says uncomfortably. And brilliantly, I might add.

Adriana searches his face. "Ahh," she says, smiling at me. "This is Desert?"

He nods.

"Miss McGraw!" She hurries to unload the bags of produce, still in her arms. She pushes it all into the fridge without special arrangement and closes the door. She wipes her hands on a towel then outstretches one. "So nice to meet you." Her eyes are like, practically twinkling.

What do I say, "Same here"? I take her hand. "Thanks."

"What brings you around? Not that you're not welcome. You're most welcome."

"Just visiting Liam."

"Ahh," she says again, nodding at me, then at Liam, then at me. Like it's slowly dawning on her that we've hooked up. "I didn't know you were such good friends."

"I told you," Liam says.

"*Verdad.* Right. Desert, let me ask you something, *mamita*. . . ."

Mamita? Like, whatever, lady!

"You don't have to answer right now, but would you do an interview with me?"

"An interview?" An interview?

"Yeah, mama, like—"

"I know what an interview is," I interrupt, not meaning to. And what's with that *mama* crap?

She laughs, then tilts her head, smiling like a Barbie doll. "Right, of course. Silly. *Verdad que* I can be silly, Liamsito?"

Liam nods, somewhat embarrassed.

I stand there, leaning on the counter, completely speechless. I haven't the faintest idea what to say to this. Nobody's ever asked *me* for an interview before. Nobody's ever cared what the kid has to say about rock 'n' roll.

She sees I'm lost for words. "Desert, don't take me the wrong way; I'm not setting out to hurt your mom, okay?"

Great. Another person not setting out to hurt Mom. But now Mom's gone, isn't she? Wandering the streets like a zombie, lost.

"I'm just concerned with parenting issues. It's the key to raising responsible kids, you know. One of the reasons our country's kids are failing miserably, emotionally—just watch the news—is poor parenting. Not that your mother is a poor parent. I'm sure she's not. But don't you wonder what you'd be like if your mom regarded you as more important than her career?"

Wow. Un-freakin'-believable of her to assume my mom thinks managing is more important than me. I haven't even agreed to an interview yet, and she's already asking dirty questions. Let me tell you what, it's a gutsy as hell question. And as much as I want to attack her for it, could she be right?

She turns around to bark at the girls, wrestling at the kitchen table over a coral-colored marker. "Carolina! Lilian! *Paren ya!*" Immediately the girls straighten up.

Whoa. Drill sergeant. "I've thought about a lot of things," I tell her. "Enough things to fill a book, but I don't know if I want the world to know."

She nods silently. Liam traces the outline of the floor tiles with his foot, listening, staying out of the way.

"It would be fascinating to see things through your point of view. Think about it, at least?"

"I will." *Mamita.*

We hang out with Liam's sisters for a while. Adriana doesn't bring up the subject again. She comments on the lack of rain, the heat, the pasta dish she's preparing for dinner. Liam doesn't mention it either. He helps Carolina draw Mickey Mouse with her markers. Lilian asks me if I'll help her draw a playground. I don't think I've ever seen a playground in real life. But I know what they look like.

And then it hits me. How sad that is. That we never had time to go to a playground. That my mom never took me, because of how busy she always was, still is. That sitting here, with these little girls, makes me feel like a big sister. This is what it feels like to have a nice, quiet afternoon at home with the family. This is *Seventh Heaven.*

To talk about it openly with Adriana, surely for a psychologist to pick apart later, now seems inviting. Healing even. Before I could flip the interview idea in my head one more time, I hear myself say, "I'll do it."

Liam looks up.

So does Adriana, over from the stove, wooden spoon stirring, eyes smiling. "Good, *mamita*. Good." She squints at the school calendar on the fridge. "How does a week from next Saturday sound?"

Chapter Twenty-Two

This interview is my chance. My chance to be heard. I've argued with Mom too many times on this subject. Between Dad's exploits and the pressure on Mom to stay home, Crossfire's sure to end.

And that's what we all need right now. A little sanity. Dad needs it. I need it. Mom needs it. Mom, especially.

Ignoring Adriana's offer to drive me home, I pace quickly through the streets. A car drives by and honks. I look over. Some creepy idiot fluttering his tongue at me. Maybe Liam's right. Maybe I need to stop walking alone. I hurry home.

Again, Dad's by himself. Mom's car is still not in the garage. I can hear a guitar in the studio. But I'm not going anywhere near it. I don't want to talk to Dad or J. C. or anybody right now. I enter my room, closing the door behind me. My computer flashes photos at me. The screensaver is set to shuffle through my digital album.

There's me and Dad, hanging out on a hotel balcony. Milan, was it? Dad and Phil, raising glasses. Mom and I, hugging. Mom and Marie, waving. I sit at the desk and watch the show for a while.

When I move the mouse, I notice new e-mail in Outlook. Among the dozens of newsletters I subscribe to, I pick out the message from Matti McGraw and click it open:

From: matildemcg@crossfire.com

To: "Desert McGraw"

Subject: I'm ok

Honey, I'm sorry I left without saying anything. I can't be around your father right now. I need some time alone. I'm at the Clevelander. Call me in Room 14. Don't worry, I'll be back soon, I'll explain everything. Two days tops, sweetie. If you can't handle Dad for two days, let me know. I'll come home. I love you.—Mom

---

I'll explain everything. That's all right, Mom. I already know everything. I try to imagine her, sitting in a dark hotel room, crying and smoking, flipping through cable channels. Watching the Food Network through tears. And it doesn't seem right. She should be here.

Two days.

I open some newsletters. Sales, Desert! Big Events, Desert!

Free Shipping, Desert, with any order over a hundred dollars!
How totally exciting! Not. I scroll through each to find the
unsubscribe link. The new mail bell pings. I haven't even found
time to sit and personalize all my sounds yet. I click over to see
the new message.

My stomach tightens. Brianna.

From: bri4nn4@stalphonsus.edu

To: "Desert McGraw"

Subject: Loser

stop emailing me, u ass. ur the one who left, right? btw retard, ur dad's
doing it with marie she talks too freakin' much now leave me the hell
alone.

My pulse. It's everywhere. Throat, fingertips on the mouse,
ankle. Blood pumping, rushing all over my body, trying to provide
oxygen, trying to save me. The flat-screen monitor, bearer of the
news, silent.

Your dad's doing it with Marie. That can't be true. She's lying.
No, she's right. Of course it's true. Why didn't I see this? Do I
hear laughing?

Marie. Doing my dad. Lying to me, to everybody. Every nerve
under my skin is alive. I want to kill something, somebody. I want
to hurt her. Them. Both of them. All of them.

*Mom? Don't cry, Mom. It's okay, Mom. Mom, please stop! Stop
crying!* Where am I?

Suddenly I'm on the monitor in a rage, hurling it away, crashing, sparks, glass on the floor. Keyboard flying, dangling off the desk. Chair, thrown against my bed, bouncing off, turning on its side. Books from the shelf, out, flinging across the room, one by one.

"Dammit!!" A voice is screaming. Mine? Can't be. "Screw all of you!! Go to hell!!"

Backpack chucked on the floor, framed photographs plucked off the wall, flung to the mirror. Glass cracking. Papers everywhere. Goldfish in the aquarium, oblivious.

I can't take this anymore! My heart, it's gonna burst. It's gonna break. It's gonna . . .

Lie down, honey. Sweetie, it's okay. Lie down. I'll be fine. Daddy loves me. I know he does. Shh, it's all right. Breathe, hon. Breathe.

It's taken me two days to find Marie. Dad hadn't spoken to her since last week, since they postponed the sessions. I figured she'd be in her condo on Collins Avenue, but she's not. She's hanging out with Faith at Max's on Ocean Drive, about three blocks down.

When Marie opens the door to my livid form, Faith bolts down the stairs, disappearing along Ocean Drive. I stand in the doorway, as expressionless as I can get. My lack of beach bag, towel, and sunscreen should indicate I didn't come to hang out with her on the sand. "How dare you." Not even a question.

"Desert—"

"Don't," I say, extremely composed. I swore to myself on the way here in Michael's car that I would *not* lose control again, no matter what. She doesn't deserve to see me lose it.

"Come in," she says, pulling back the door.

"I only came to tell you something."

"Come in and tell me," she urges, gesturing inside.

"No."

Marie stands there, sarong and linen shirt over a swimmer's one-piece. Her eyes are swollen. She's been crying. Good.

"Suit yourself," she says, rubbing her tired face.

I can feel my heart quickening again, veins expanding, lungs fighting collapse. *Deep breath, Desert. Deep breath.* My fist squeezes against my thigh. "Stay away from my father."

A gust of breath escapes her, almost a laugh. "Really? That's what you came to tell me? Stay away from your father?" Her lean on the door gets a little too comfortable. "Or what?"

"Or there's no telling what I might do to you."

"Is that right?" She obviously thinks I'm joking.

"Yes, that's right."

"Desert, honey—"

"Don't call me honey, you lying, scheming—"

"Excuse me!" she interrupts, holding up her stupid hand. "But I do believe you know nothing about the situation."

"I know enough. I know you betrayed us, me, my mom, just to be with my dad, and for what? For sex? You are such a tremendous loser!"

"No, Desert, not just for sex. For love, okay?"

Love. Like she even knows what that means. "You're mental, you know that? My dad doesn't love you. He loves my mom. He

167

loves me, J. C., Max, Phil, Ryan, the music. Not you."

"He told me so," she says, almost like a child.

This is news to me. Could that even be true? I mean—as a friend, I've always known that. But as more?

Marie sighs, leaning her head on the door, staring past me at the palms. Their long shadows sway on her figure. "He said he did. We were together for four months, Desert."

"When?"

"During the last recording. It wasn't just a night, or a mistake. He told me he loved me. Then he ended it—the day of the new release."

Why do I care about these details anyway? It doesn't matter anymore. Mom slashed her off the payroll last night. "Yeah, and you know why? Because he didn't. He didn't love you. He probably didn't even know why he said it. He was confused."

"I'm not so sure about that, Desi."

Desi. What a lie. What a freakin' lie of a name. How dare she use it. "Don't call me that."

"You're upset. You have every right to be, but you have to believe me, your dad had an equal part in this."

"I know my dad had an equal part in this!" I scream, and a couple of faces peer out down the hall. "What does that have to do with anything? But you, Marie! How dare you? How dare you tell me that everything you were doing, with Adriana, by hiring the photographer, hiring Faith, all those things. How could you tell me you were doing it for me? You lied!"

She stands there, quiet. Our eyes, locked.

"Stay away from my dad. That's all I came to say." I walk away, toward the outside stairs.

By the time I reach them, I can hear her crying. Her sniffs sound odd, unfamiliar. I've never known Marie like this. When she begins speaking again, I pause. "In the end he refused me, Desert. Unless you've been cast aside when you love someone, love them so much your heart can crumble just by imagining them gone from your life, unless you know what that's like, you can't judge me, you hear?"

Silence. The heads down the hall are actually listening. "What?!" I shout at the audience, and they retreat, slamming doors.

"You don't know what it's like," she goes on. "If he thought he could just play with my emotions like that, leading me to think we would someday have something, then ignore me on a new day—I wasn't going to let him get away with that. He had to go down."

And there it is. The ugly truth. That's why she did it all. To hurt him. For hurting her. Eye for an eye. In the face of rejection, I can't think of a more immature way to respond.

I see Liam watching me from the car, worried expression. I start down the steps again, leaving her behind for good. "Go to hell, Marie."

The ride home seems long. No one speaks; no one dares. But my brain is screaming. So I do the only thing I know how to shut it up.

until you've walked that mile in my shoes
until you've seen my pain
Don't even pretend to know me at all
Don't even claim to know my game
I don't know what's worse, your betrayal or my trust
In you, because I wanted to, because I felt I must
And you laughed in my face, you laughed in it hard
But I'll turn my cheek, try to disregard
your foolish attempt to fracture this whole
This family, this love, that you tried to control
Leave me here to repair the wounds you made
In your joke, in your game, in your masquerade

Chapter Twenty-Three

Halloween. What a totally useless holiday. Exactly why should we celebrate the dead? I've had enough of walking into Eckerd's, finding black-and-orange aisles full of crappy candy, adhesive for gluing fake scars to one's forehead, and cheap plastic masks. Plus, why do people feel the need to pressure us anti-Halloweenists to participate in stupid costume parties? I do not care to humiliate myself in front of others.

So rather than attend the Palm Grove Monster Bash or accompany Liam and his little sisters on a trick-or-treat hunt, Becca and I are home tonight, watching monster movie marathons—the one and only great thing about Halloween.

After I trashed my room last weekend, all has somewhat stabilized on the home front. Mom's been home. Quiet, but home.

Dad's been really nice to everyone. Quiet, but nice. They've been civil. Pissed, but civil. A miracle in itself. Me, I don't get a new monitor for a while, until I learn to manage my anger in more resourceful ways.

But I'm not the same. I can't tell you for sure what it is, but I'm not. Still angry, maybe? Don't know. Cynical? I was already cynical before the Marie Episode. Empty? Yeah, empty maybe.

On the floor Becca eats popcorn, watching TV and using my bed as a backrest. I'm on the bed, nabbing popcorn out of the bowl. *Creature from the Black Lagoon* coming up next. Awesome. That movie's the best. I love the way the gill dude walks with his arms out, trying to catch Julia Adams, like an amphibious Frankenstein. The whole thing's so stupid, it's good.

"I can't believe Marie was trying to break up Crossfire, just to get back at your dad," Becca reflects during a commercial.

"I know, right?"

"Do you think it worked?" she asks.

"Things don't look good, Beck."

Becca sulks for a while. "I don't know what I'd do if they broke up, Des," she says finally. "I look forward to the next set release, just to help me keep coping."

"You'd manage. You don't have any other choice. What would you've done about Marie?" I ask, changing the subject. Becca takes this whole Crossfire thing way too seriously.

"Don't know. Probably the same thing you did. I'm surprised you didn't break her legs, after what you did to your computer."

My poor monitor. Look at it there in its box, its coffin. The glass had been everywhere. I hadn't realized how hard I threw it. In fact, I don't remember all that much. I only remember seeing red and feeling blood rushing, hearing it in my ears, in my head. I felt like some kind of animal.

Universal Studios presents . . .

"I can't believe Jessie cut you loose like that," I say, changing the subject. Although I totally believe it. She was so obviously using her.

"Whatever."

Richard Carlson . . . Julia Adams . . . in a Jack Arnold film . . .

We watch the movie in silence for a while. At the next commercial break I ask, "But seriously Becca, didn't you see it coming?"

"Huh?" She leans her head back to see me upside down.

"Couldn't you tell Jessie was totally using you to gain some access?"

"Someone's getting a little snobby," she says, holding the popcorn bowl up on her shoulder for me to reach into.

Snobby? Surely she doesn't mean me. "It has nothing to do with being snobby, Beck. Anyone could see it, ask Liam."

Her head straightens up. Her eyes blaze, questioning me. "Why should I ask Liam?"

"Because. He didn't like her either."

"Is that right? Then why the hell didn't anyone inform me of this? You guys are supposed to be watching my back, not talking behind it. Dammit."

She sets down the bowl, gets up, and tramps to my bathroom.

I can hear her using the toilet, yanking toilet paper angrily, washing her hands. Then she pulls the door open, hard.

"Look, for your four-one-one, I thought Jessie really liked me, okay?" she says, standing in the doorway. Looks like the tears are on their way.

"Movie's back on," I say. The boat glides slowly on the water's surface, while unbeknownst to its crew, a creature lurks in the lagoon. "Look, what do I know?" I tell her. "Maybe she did for a while, but you're better off without her, trust me." I toss kernels around in the ceramic bowl, hearing them clink over and over again.

From the depths of the murky water in Wakulla Springs, Florida, comes a creature unknown to mankind, a creature so fierce, so hideous, so absolutely horrifying, he has to wear a rubber suit.

"I'm better off without her?" Becca hisses.

Darn, and I thought she was finished. I look up to find her still standing there, mouth open. I thought she was watching the flick, not obsessing over what I'd said.

"Yeah, Becca, it's good that you found this out early, before you invested any more time in her. Or would you rather have found out a year from now that she was a total wench?"

Yikes. Not good. Becca could not look any scarier. I think the Halloween spirits have possessed her, and now she's about to lash out at me, her only friend besides Liam to ever take her in. Why is she making such a big deal about this? Everyone gets dumped at least once.

"You're incredible, you know that?" she pretty much spits. "Thanks for your sympathy! What did you know about Jessie anyway? Nothing. You never even gave her a chance."

"I did give her a chance. She blew it. She asked to meet Flesh. But I told her no. I told her no because I wasn't going to let her mooch off you like that. That's all she wanted you for. *She* dumped *you*, Becca, not the other way around."

"Yeah? Well, it still hurts! I thought she cared for me. I thought she appreciated me." Becca wipes her tears.

"She was using you."

"Fine, but you don't have to call her a wench. She's still a nice person."

"If you say so." That's not what Liam's heard on campus, but whatever. "I just thought you were mad at her. Sorry."

"Well, I'm mad it didn't work out, I'm mad she wasn't the one, I'm mad that my supposed friends thought she was worthless and didn't bother to tell me anything. Yeah, I'm mad, but not at Jessie."

Enough already. We're supposed to be leaning on each other tonight. God, Becca sulks like no other!

"Becca, I'm sorry. I didn't mean anything bad by that, okay? I'm just trying to make you feel better. It's moping night, isn't it? Here, watching cheesy movies, eating popcorn, drinking carbonated crap, isn't that what we agreed to do tonight?"

"Yes, but you don't have to insult anybody."

"But that's half the fun!" If she takes me seriously, I'm gonna go postal on her.

She sits back down. I never know how Becca's going to take something. She pretends to watch the movie, but I can tell her mind's going a hundred miles an hour. She's trying to figure out her life, trying to understand how anyone could get sick of her excessively negative attitude. Imagine that.

What she needs is a little perspective. "At least you didn't have to go through what I went through this week. What I'm still going through. What I'll continue to go through, at least until my parents patch things up," I offer.

And by the eerie silence in the room, except for the sound of Wakulla Springs bubbles, swishing of water, and the chirping of B-grade studio birds coming from the TV, I'd say I just lit a short fuse.

Becca turns around and glares. I mean, glares, like shooting daggers, like she could never think of anything strong enough to say to warrant the hatred she has for me at this moment.

"You know what your problem is?" she asks, all cool suddenly.

This should be interesting. I've always wanted to see Becca's view of my shortcomings. "No, why don't you tell me?" I say, sitting up and crossing my arms.

"I think I will." Her voice is calm, but her eyes well up, betraying her. "Your problem is you think you've got everybody figured out, and everything's always about you, isn't it? You can't see past your nose to save your life."

"Oo, scary!" I pretend to shiver. She can do better, I hope.

"And you're too self-involved to listen to anyone else's goddamned ideas."

You mean Becca has goddamned ideas beyond her brooding silence? "Please, enlighten me," I say, noticing the striking resemblance between her and the swamp creature on the screen behind her.

"Yeah, so your dad cheated on your mom, with her best friend even. That definitely sucks."

She can't even begin to understand this one. "Sucks" is an understatement.

"But guess what?" she continues. "At least he didn't run off, leaving you and your mom behind. At least he ended things with Marie. Do you think it's easy for him? With his job and all?"

That's it, if she even thinks for one second . . . "Don't defend what he did, Becca!" I shout. "Forget Flesh for one freakin' second, will you? As my dad, as anybody's dad, what he did was wrong! Okay? Wrong!" How anyone can ever think rock 'n' roll behavior is permissible is beyond me.

"I'm not defending what he did. Yeah, it was wrong, but at least he acted responsibly enough afterward to try and fix what he did. Because he loves you!"

This is true.

"At least *your* dad loves you!" She's screaming. Becca's screaming. At me. How weird. And now she's crying. God, I didn't remember about her dad. Maybe I do need to see past my little circle. Damn.

Becca stands and starts gathering her things. I guess she's not going to stay overnight then. She pauses by the TV, wiping her eyes. "He's still home, isn't he? Your dad?"

I guess. He could've taken off. He could've stayed with Marie, or any of the other thousands of women who've offered themselves to him over the years, even. But I say nothing.

"And then there's your mom!"

You mean she's not finished? I think I've had enough of this abuse!

"Your poor mom, sacrificing herself, taking nasty criticism, all so you can grow up with two loving parents by your side, not some nanny! She's done everything to keep you comfortable and satisfied, even on the road. But no! You're too much of a selfish brat to see any of this, aren't you? 'I'm on the road too much, everyone caters to my needs too much, my life sucks!'" she says, flailing her arms like a baby.

Is that supposed to be me she's imitating? I don't whine that way!

"And! Oh, wait, and . . . !" She pauses to laugh, but it's a crazy laugh, and I get the feeling what's coming isn't all that funny. "You have a boyfriend who's nice to you, who does anything to please you! Jesus! Can someone please tell me where the line starts for these free giveaways?" She looks around, like she's expecting the photos on the walls to answer.

Great tantrum. I'd say she's ranting almost as good as me. I just can't bring myself to interrupt her.

"You think your worst problem is your beautiful name and that your life isn't all perfect, like that stupid TV show."

"*Seventh Heaven.*"

"Whatever! God! Well, you know what? Define 'perfect,' poor little rock star's kid! If I had your life, I'd make your parents proud. But that'll never happen, now will it?"

I could answer, pull anything out of my deep reservoir of sarcastic wit, but why bother? She won't be around to hear it. Becca could care less.

She crosses the room, grabs her bag and her guitar. Then she pauses at the door. "I can't take this life anymore. I won't be back," she announces through sobs. Then she's gone, leaving nothing behind but me.

And the Creature from the Black Lagoon.

Chapter Twenty-Four

If there's anything that should take my mind off Becca right now, it's Liam's half-naked body in my pool. His bathing suit hangs low on his hips, so those abs I was talking about are in their full glory. But unfortunately, I can't stop thinking about the little brat.

"I swear, it was like she was possessed by someone else, Liam. She totally went ballistic on me." I tell him about last night while wading in the shallow end, wishing I had the nerve to run my hands down that stomach of his.

He's listening, but he's also stealing glances at me as I glide by. I may not be Barbie in a bikini, but I guess I shouldn't complain. Liam seems to appreciate me just fine. And from the artwork I saw in his bedroom, I don't think I have to worry about looking any particular way.

"What else did she say?" he asks, his finger drawing curvy lines on the surface of the water.

"Well, let's see . . . that I'm unappreciative, that my dad deserves respect even though he cheated on my mom, that my mom is the best, that you're nice to me, that I'm unappreciative—"

"You said that already."

"That I'm a jerk for not giving Jessie a chance."

"That girl was using her."

I look up at him. "That's what I told her!"

"Yeah, but I told you you can't say that to Becca, remember? She doesn't take criticism well. Look, Des, you know how Becca can be really negative sometimes."

"Sometimes? Try all the time."

"Right, well, you gotta take it easy on her. She can get really down on herself."

"I know this, Liam. Anyone who thinks they're invisible to the world has got to be pretty down on themselves."

I let myself slide under the surface for a few seconds, then pop back up. When I wipe the water from my eyes, I see Liam smiling. "Um . . . what?" I ask.

He shrugs and looks down. "Nothing."

"Nothing?" *Yeah, okay, buddy.*

He bugs his eyes out. "Nothing!"

"Okay, then." *Whatever you say.*

"You just look hot when you do that, that's all."

To which I freeze. I mean, what do I say to that? "Thanks."

"You're welcome." He grins.

"Um. So anyway . . . that time I told you about? When Becca said Crossfire's music is the only thing that keeps her going, I was like, *'What?'* Why would someone say that?"

He backs up and leans against the edge of the pool, arms stretched out. "Why? Because she's depressed, Des."

"Yeah, no kidding, she's depressed. You should've seen how she got when I told her that Crossfire's future didn't look so hot."

"No, you're not understanding." He reaches back to support his weight then hoists himself out of the pool, water spilling onto the baked brick. "I mean she really is depressed. As in, depression. As in, she takes medication."

I stop and focus on him. He's gotta be kidding me. The only other person I know that takes meds for that is J. C. Funny, too, because Becca sometimes reminds me of him.

Liam sees I'm stunned into silence. "Yeah. You're not supposed to know that, though."

Well, I guess that explains a thing or two. "But she's told me other things that you'd think are a bigger deal."

"What, about being gay? That's nothing. It's the whole deal with her dad not wanting her, her mom's dead, her sister's away. And her grandmother—the woman's like eighty-something, and you name it, she's got it . . . high-blood pressure . . . high cholesterol. She's not gonna be around forever."

Man. Talk about getting dealt a crappy hand. I look away and see my parents sitting out on the deck. Mom's on the left feeding seagulls, Dad's on the right checking out boats. They're not talking, but they're there. I don't know what I'd do if *one* of them was gone, much less both of them.

Behind me, I can feel Liam watching me watching them. He sighs. "Did he tell her, or did she find out?"

I haven't asked my mom anything about the affair, because I honestly don't want to know, but *that*, I did ask. And it just might be the reason why I still see my dad as a good person, even though he's a bonehead. The fact that it was him who came clean makes a world of difference. *"He* told *her."*

After Liam leaves, after my shower, I feel something inside me breaking down. And all of a sudden, I'm leaning over the sink, crying. I think of my mom and all she's been through, my dad and how difficult it must've been for him to make a mistake and admit it, of Becca and her laundry list of cruel life events, how she thinks she's invisible. God, I couldn't see anything that was happening. How could I be so freakin' blind to everything?

I rush into my room and dial Becca's number. I don't know how to come right out and say I'm sorry. Isn't that kind of dorky? *You're supposed to look humble, Desert. That's the whole idea.* Then, I'll ask how she's been and stuff. And hopefully, she'll still want to be friends with me. Hopefully.

Her phone keeps ringing on and on, though. No voice mail. No answering machine. I'll guess I'll just talk to her at school on Monday.

Chapter Twenty-Five

"Rebecca Reese?"

No answer.

"Miss Reese?"

Nada.

I look at the empty seat next to me. "She's not here," I say. Neither is Ms. Smigla. Her sub, Mr. Perez, marks the grade book. After taking roll, he makes it clear we are not to open our mouths, just read from *Romeo and Juliet*. He takes all the fun out of having a substitute.

> *Two households, both alike in dignity,*
> *In fair Verona, where we lay our scene,*
> *From ancient grudge break to new mutiny,*

Where civil blood makes civil hands unclean.
From forth the fatal loins of these two foes
A pair of star-crost lovers take their life;
Whose misadventured piteous overthrows
Doth with their death bury their parents' strife.

Parents' strife. Ha! What would I do to bury my parents' strife? Anything, probably. Maybe Becca's right. My parents have done a lot for me. I never said they didn't. I just wanted more. What's so bad about wanting more? I don't think that's so selfish. She didn't have to call me selfish.

Liam looks at me over his shoulder. I wish I could sit with him.

The fearful passage of their death-mark'd love,
And the continuance of their parents' rage

Parents' rage. Desert's rage. Becca's rage. A folded note drops into my view. I open it to see Liam's handwriting.

Have you heard from Becca? Do you know if she's here?

I write back.

Obviously she's not here! you mean is she somewhere else in the school building? I don't know. I tried calling her all weekend, but she wasn't home.

I slide the note onto Carlos's shoulder, the dude sitting in front of me who delivered Liam's note. He passes it forward. Not a minute later Carlos sighs heavily, flinging the note back at me.

I called her too, and didn't get through. Could her sister be in town or something?

My pen scribbles fast.

Maybe she's sick

Fling note forth. Carlos is ready to shove the note up my ass. Ten seconds later, fling back.

Becca doesn't miss school for anything. Can you call her from your cell?

yeah, after class. you know what was really weird that I didn't tell you? when she left that night, she was all, "I can't take this life, blah, blah. I won't be back." real dramatic, like smigla

She said that? She actually said, "I can't take this life? I won't be back"?

Yeah, and once she even said, "sometimes I think of ending things."

Carlos turns around, flinging Liam's reply at me for the last time. "Use the phone," he mouths.

Dammit Desert!!! When the bell rings, follow me to the car.

Thirty minutes later, after first period ends, Liam and I hustle through the halls. A few people hand us flyers about a weekend party. We breeze by them, drop the sheets in the stairwell, pass the cafeteria. The school security guard is flirting with a senior cheerleader. Loser. He doesn't even blink when we sneak behind him.

Outside there's a light drizzle falling. The rain hits the cars in the parking lot with a sleepy sound. "Liam, what is it? You think she'd do something stupid?"

His lips press together as he tows me by the hand. "She said all that? About ending things, and she wouldn't be back?"

"I think that's what she said. I remember it was so melodramatic, but I guess she was pissed. You know, she was just overreacting."

"How do you know she was overreacting? How do you know she didn't mean it? *Coño*, Des." He shakes his head, weaving between cars to his brother's Integra.

What the hell's this third degree all about? "What? *Coño*, what?"

Liam's voice is deeper than usual, darker. "Don't you know what to look out for when someone like Becca . . . forget it, you can be so clueless sometimes."

"Oh, so now I'm clueless? Don't you get mad at me, Liam! I don't even know what you're talking about."

"Desert!" He stops and jerks my shoulders to face him, scaring me. "When I told you the other day about Becca being depressed, clinically depressed, the fact that she said she thought of killing herself, then said good-bye, should've been a huge red flag to you!" He's shouting. Now Liam's shouting.

"She never said it like that!" I cry. Actually she might've said it like that. She said Crossfire is the only thing that keeps her going. I thought she meant like, figuratively, or something. "Liam, she was probably just saying it for attention!"

"Really?" He flips his palms up, questioning. "How the hell do you know that? How do you know she didn't mean it? I didn't know you were qualified to make that judgment! Where the hell does it say, 'Desert, Little Miss Ph.D.,' on your shirt?" Then, he walks off, leaving me there like an idiot.

I can't believe all this. I can't believe now Liam's ragging on me. Am I really that stupid? I run after him. What else did Becca say? *Think, Desert, think.* Her mom dies, her dad leaves her, the girl she really digs dumps her, plus she tells me all these depressing things. Then Liam tells me it's real, that she sees a doctor for it.

You know what? I *am* pretty freakin' stupid. "Liam, I didn't see the whole picture like that! I didn't realize!" I call after him.

We reach the car just as the rain begins to pour down. "Why didn't you tell me any of that before? Damn!" He throws his arm up, unarms the alarm, and yanks the door open. "We gotta find her."

"I didn't think it was that big a deal. I didn't see it like that, I didn't realize," I ramble, getting into the passenger seat. "I wouldn't have let her go if I'd seen it that way. My mom drove her home, but I wouldn't have let her go pissed like that if I'd known. Oh, God."

Liam's not talking to me. His eyes are fierce, focused on the wet road.

I deserve every shitty thing that ever happens to me for not seeing the signs. But at least I called her after what Liam told me, didn't I? I wanted to show her I was still her friend, that I was sorry. At least I'm not a *total* craphead.

I wipe wet mascara off my eyelashes with the inside of my shirt. A thought of Becca, lying on the bathroom floor, surrounded by blood, flashes through my head. Another one of her outstretched arm, still gripping a bottle of sleeping pills. And yet another of her pale face, eyes open. Stop it, brain, stop!

"God, please let her be okay, God, please!"

Liam speeds down Palm Avenue, cornering onto Hibiscus, winding through the set of narrow roads that make up Coconut Grove around our school. Lots of cops in this area. Don't any of them see us cruising through all these red lights? I swear, if anything's happened to Becca, I think I'll hurt myself, too. This is all my fault, totally and completely my fault.

"Please, God, please." Since when do I pray so much? *Please don't let there be anything unusual going at her house. I beg you. I'll do anything you ask of me. Anything!*

We wind into her neighborhood, where some little kids are riding bikes in the rain. Shouldn't they be in school? Liam makes another turn, screeching onto Becca's street, hauling ass over the speed bumps. At the end of the road, sure enough, there's a group of three or four people standing in the street, talking under a cluster of umbrellas. My stomach squeezes, heart pounds hard. But we can't see Becca's house yet, not until we reach the corner. When Liam makes the last turn, the house comes into view, and we spot them—what we hoped wouldn't be there—the flashing lights.

Red and white. Red and white. Silent.

Something inside me breaks down. A feeling washes through, not like the rage from reading Brianna's e-mail, but something else. Something more painful. I don't think I've ever cried like this. My heart, it hurts. Guilt. This is called guilt.

As Liam pulls up to the house, the sirens begin to wail.

And the ambulance takes off.

Chapter Twenty-Six

Liam yanks the emergency brake, throws open the door, jumps out, all before the car even comes to a full stop. "Didi, what's going on?" he yells at a shivering woman, crying, underneath an umbrella. "Is she all right?"

I stay in the car, head down, unable to look up. I can't. I can't look at anyone right now. This is my fault. All my fault.

I hear the woman reply, "No, dear, they're taking her to Mercy."

Oh, no! They're taking her to Mercy! "What's Mercy?" I ask Liam.

He ignores me.

"Who?" Liam asks stupidly. So stupid of him! The car hums in idle, air conditioner ticking erratically. Tears drip into my hair.

"Edith, sweetheart. Edie!" shouts the lady, trying to be heard over the growing downpour.

"Edie?" I look up at the woman, examine the pink, spongy rollers in her hair, the tan, leathery skin. "Who's Edie?" I ask.

Are we on the wrong street? This is Becca's house, isn't it?

"Don't you know? Why are you here, then?" she asks me, rubbing her arm, warming herself in the humid air. "Are you lost?"

Liam turns and hangs from the car door, his face hidden by his arms. His hair, shirt, soaked. Water drips from his nose and chin. He gathers his breath, slowly, recuperating. A half-laugh, half-cry escapes his lips. "Her grandmother, Des. Becca's grandmother, Edie."

"Oh!" Sweet Jesus. *Becca's grandmother, Edie.* I never even knew her name. Never even met her. "Is she all right? What about Becca?"

Liam nods, face still hidden.

I think I'm going to faint. I roll down the window to take in the cool breezes. Rain washes my face, rinses me. It feels wonderful, refreshing. Becca's okay, but her grandmother's not.

"What happened to her? To Edie?" I ask.

Didi, with the pink, spongy rollers, shakes her head as she talks. "She hadn't been feeling well since Saturday, didn't want to eat hardly a bite all weekend. Then this morning she started complaining of chest pains, so we called her doctor."

Liam stands up straight and faces her. His clothes are soaked, his hair smushed against his face. I think he lost his voice.

"Oh, honey, get out of the rain," Didi says, waving her hand around. Liam slumps into the car seat. She waddles up to him, covering the open door space with her umbrella.

Poor Becca! Now her grandmother's sick. Great. If anything happens to Edie, then Becca will have no one but her sister, who lives somewhere else. No wonder she feels the way she does half the time. No wonder she's the all-time moping queen of Miami. Suddenly the idea of her taking solace in my dad's songs doesn't sound so ridiculous. I can see it. And I always waved it away like it was no big deal.

"Was Becca in there?" Liam asks, pointing in the direction the ambulance left.

"Yes, hon. I'm gonna go inside and get dressed. They've got to let me in at the hospital. Becca shouldn't be alone."

"We'll take you, if you want," Liam offers. He's so sweet. So damn sweet. I didn't even think of that.

"Oh, dear, thank you. That might be better. Don't know if I can drive right now. Give me a minute to get changed, will you? Wait in the car. Don't get out in this rain."

Didi disappears up the slick path to her house, while Liam and I stay in the car, breathless, speechless.

At Mercy Hospital, we sit inside the emergency waiting room. Liam already called his mom and the school to let them know where we were. The secretary actually told him that next time we should go by the office first and receive permission to leave school grounds. Can you believe that? Emergencies are called emergencies for a reason, people!

On the TV, suspended from the ceiling, some Spanish talk

show host is trying to calm down an angry audience member. Looks like he doesn't like the gay couple embracing their baby. They're well-dressed, seem like loving dads, and the baby looks happy too. But the guy's going off on them. I don't know what he's saying, but who cares? They love her! Isn't that all that matters?

Isn't it? At least they love her and want her. . . .

Thoughts of Becca run through my mind again, and I find myself crying. Again. Liam, for the first time since we left school, pats my back to comfort me, but it's not the same. Maybe he's still mad.

"Desert," he says.

Sniff.

"You know this isn't over, right?"

I look at him. "What do you mean?"

"I mean, it's good that Becca didn't hurt herself, but now's when we really have to keep an eye on her. Now that this has happened."

He's right. If this doesn't annihilate Becca, I don't know what will. All we need now is for Crossfire to break up and clinch it.

The man sitting next to me is sniffing. I wonder if he lost someone. I wonder if he just lost the most important person left in his life. And that lady over there, the one who's studying the floor so hard, what's she thinking? Probably waiting patiently for some news. Bad news. What anguish. Thank God I've never lost anyone close to me. There was Grandma and Grandpa, but I was so young when they both died. I don't really remember.

"Liam," I say, trying to think of something worth saying next. I really shouldn't be talking at all. I've done enough damage. "I'm so sorry."

For a moment he's quiet, opening and closing a brochure on first aid. Then, he sighs. "Desert, look, just forget it. We both should've paid closer attention to her, including me. I'm sorry I got mad at you."

That was easy. Why can't I apologize like that? We sit in silence another minute. "Man, we've already been here two hours. What's going on in there?" I try to look through the double doors to the ER.

"I guess they have to stabilize her," Liam says.

We watch the Spanish talk show to the end, until the camera pans across the five gay couples and their children, adopted or artificially conceived, and the audience claps heartily, some waving at the camera. The credits roll.

"Hey, guys." Becca's behind us.

"Hey!" We stand to greet her.

Liam hugs her hard. "Beck, are you all right? How's your grandma?"

She wipes her nose with a tissue. "She's okay for now. It was a mild heart attack. They've got her on some medication to thin her blood. Didi's in there with her."

"Didi and Edie," Liam says, smiling.

"Didi and Edie," Becca repeats. Must be some kind of inside joke.

Then she gives me a look that could mean I'm sorry, or come here you idiot, or something else, and reaches for me.

"Becca, I'm really sorry," I say pathetically. As if that could really comfort her right now. "We thought you were hurt. We thought . . . " Should I say it? What we feared? "You were dead."

"What?" She chuckles softly. "Why?"

Liam raises his eyebrows and tilts his head at me. Yes, he'd like to know why as well.

"Oh . . . um . . . well." It's moments like these when I'm at my verbal best. "We thought maybe you had hurt yourself. You know."

"Hurt myself. You mean, killed myself?" she asks, glancing around to see if anyone is overhearing this absurdity.

She said it, not me. "Well, yeah. You've been really down on yourself lately, like since I've known you."

I look at Liam. Can I get a little support here, before I make a complete fool out of myself? My mental message obviously does not get through, since Liam remains quiet.

"You've said that sometimes you wanted to end things, and well, you've been crying a lot," I add.

"Yeah, I know. I'm trying not to. But that doesn't mean I'm gonna kill myself, guys. I mean—"

"We didn't know that," Liam finally interrupts.

Becca pauses. Liam, who she's loved like a brother since the fourth grade, is saying it, so it must be true. If Desert says anything, it's a pile of crap. But hey, at least she's listening.

He goes on. "You've got problems, but you're not the only one.

I've got 'em, Desert's got 'em. . . . You gotta lean on us more, Beck."

"Well, she tried," I say, remembering my wonderful attitude Halloween night. I look at her eyes, sad and green. "But I guess I just didn't realize you've been in so much pain. Or I didn't want to see it, or something. I dunno. I'm sorry, Beck. I'm sorry I was such an ass."

Becca sighs and sits down. Her head falls into her lap. When she comes up for air, she's got tears everywhere. "What's gonna happen now? What if she dies? What do I do? Where do I go?"

"She's not gonna die." I sit and put my arm around her. "She's gonna come out okay, you'll see." I hope to God I'm right. Because if anything does happen to Edie, Becca will have to find someone to watch her, someone to care for her. At least I've never had to worry about that. I've always had someone. Lots of some-ones. Always.

Chapter Twenty-Seven

Mangrove Cemetery. So that's what this place is called. I couldn't see the sign when I came here that night with Liam. I like Moonlit Park better.

I need to be alone for a while before this interview today. Just me and my notebook. This thing with Becca this week freaked me out. How I thought I'd lost her. It's funny how just imagining life without someone you care about can make you appreciate things more. I can't imagine what I'd do if I lost either one of my parents. Even Max, Phil, or J. C., for that matter.

Look at all these graves. There are people buried under here. Well, the remains of people anyway. I wonder if any of them took their own lives. I wonder if any of them felt invisible, like they could disappear for a few days and no one would notice.

Isn't it weird how we come into this life, and everybody goes gaga over us, showering us with attention, taking endless photos, video, and all that? Then some years go by, and well, you're just not as cute or interesting anymore, and people just stop paying attention? Why bother recording? It was only funny when she did it the first time. Weird, right, how some people can just stop caring like that?

That's how Becca feels sometimes, like nobody cares about her. I have to remind her every day if necessary. That I do care. That she's my best friend. Not some leech.

What a beautiful day, after having dismal rain all week long. The ground's still wet, brown leaves plastered into mush every-where. The smell of rotting foliage, dampness in the air. From this bench the cemetery grounds look a bit like the countries on a globe, green and brown patches. Well, if you blur your vision really, really hard, it does. I guess if you blur your eyesight hard enough, you can see anything you want.

Flesh, lead singer of Crossfire, is a god? Okay, if you say so. Jessie loved you? Sure, why not? Marie was a trusted friend? Of course she was. That's what we all wanted to believe, so it became real. We think whatever we want to think, to stay happy and calm. I guess reality's really nothing but our own version of the truth, right?

And what is the truth? My truth, anyway? Adriana's going to ask what it's been like in my situation. What should I say, that my life sucks? That having two parents who love me is really the crappiest thing that could happen to someone? How horrible it's been having a name like Desert that sets me apart from all the Billys and Amys out there? That my life's been hell, when other people, like Becca, dream of nothing but the life I have? Sometimes I forget what I'm fighting for. What *am* I fighting for?

I don't know if I can do this anymore.

Blur my eyes and faces change
Loving smiles to frightening grins
Squint hard enough and grasses turn
From palest lime to greens that burn
I blur my eyes and people seem
However dark or bright I deem
I am a victim, I am a muse
I am whatever role I choose.

Chapter Twenty-Eight

Click.

"Could you please state your name?"

"Desert." Like the sandy place with the camels.

"Last name?"

"McGraw."

The tape recorder winds, its little spokes rotating slowly.

"Desert, thank you for joining me today. I know this isn't your territory, so I appreciate it."

She sounds so formal. No *mamitas* today.

"Thanks for having me."

"We at *Tropical Home Life* aim to preserve what we consider to be the most fundamental institution, critical to human moral development, and that is the basic family unit. You've been raised in the most unusual of situations. Can you please tell us a little bit about it?"

Sigh.

"Let's see, what do you want to know? I was born in New York, raised on various planes, in buses, hotel rooms, parks, cities, rest stops. My father is Richard McGraw, Flesh, lead singer of the rock band Crossfire. My mother is Matti Thomas McGraw, the band's manager for the past seventeen years. My parents are wonderful people, but they make their mistakes like anybody else," I say, looking Adriana straight in the eye.

"Of course," she says, "of course. We'll get to their roles as parents in a moment. Tell me, what has it been like for you? You're seventeen?"

"Sixteen. I turn seventeen next month."

"Sixteen, I'm sorry. What has it been like for you, a young woman in the formative years of her life, growing up without a central location, a nucleus if you will, a place to call home, a school or community to grow up in? That must be very difficult."

Here we go. This is where I should dis my parents, the part where five days ago, I would've felt like it was my God-given right to whine for a more normal existence. But I can't do it. I just can't. "It's been great, actually."

Adriana stares at me, unblinking. Then she looks down at her clipboard, the list of questions. Nope, "It's been great," is not in the script.

"Great?" she repeats, like she misheard.

Now she'll really think I'm a freak. But you know what? I don't care anymore. I could care less what she thinks. This is how it is, how I see it now.

"Yes. I know my life's not typical. I didn't take naps in a nursery when I was a baby. I never had a playground or playmates to visit every day. I didn't take Mommy and Me classes at the Y. But I did sleep in a baby sling against my mom's chest while she worked. I went to parks, gardens, museums, landmarks, every place you can think of. It's kinda like having the world for a playground or classroom. And I never needed *Sesame Street*. Who needs Big Bird when you have three goofs like my dad's bandmates, friends, trying to make me laugh all the time?"

I remember Max years ago, jumping on Phil's back, riding horsy through the halls, then coming around to pick me up. Bubbling and giggling, I'd bounce around on Max's back while he squished Phil to death. And Dad taking pictures of the whole thing.

I'm giggling aloud, but Adriana doesn't think it's all that funny. "Is that right? So your parents' idea of fun for their child was to expose her to rock musicians and the lives they lead, including, quite possibly, alcohol and drug use?"

"Nobody ever used drugs in my presence."

"In sixteen years nobody modeled self-destructive behavior in front of you?"

"Everybody has a drink now and then, but I wouldn't call that self-destructive. I'm sure you do too, when you're not working, right?"

"I'll ask the questions."

"A few people drink heavily, but not everyone does. Not my dad, anyway. Not my mom. And to answer your question, if anyone used drugs, I was never aware of it. They never did it in front of me. They're musicians, Adriana, not idiots. Many of them are responsible."

"Responsible?" she asks, with a sarcastic laugh. "I'd be more than happy to show you a list of names of rock 'n' roll casualties, men and women both, who've lost their lives to excess in the music business, starting with Don Hynd."

What? I can't believe her. I haven't heard that name in years. How dare she bring it up?

"Your father's former drummer was found in his hotel suite, dead from a drug overdose, is this not correct?" she asks.

I shift in my seat. "Yeah, but—"

"And you were only a year old at the time, taking a nap just down the hall, is this right?"

"I think so . . . but—"

"So would you say you were brought up in an environment conducive to stability, health, and all that is necessary for a child your age?"

"Listen," I say, stopping her from starting a bloodbath. "That was a long time ago. They were young. And it was Don's mistake, not anybody else's. All my parents could do was make sure to hire someone better next time around, someone who'd be willing to work hard, not someone with a chemical dependency. Which they did. Max."

Max is the best!

"Okay, but the fact remains that you were raised at the core of the music business, surrounded by lots of other people with the same problem."

"You're right. I'm sure there *are* lots of people with the same problem. But there's also lots of people *not* in the music business who've died from drug abuse. It's not just rock stars who are self-destructing."

"But isn't self-destruction an integral part of the rock star's image?"

"Why would you say that? Rebellion is what rock 'n' roll's all about, not irresponsibility." She knows nothing about musicians. And I thought she did her homework.

"But being irresponsible goes hand in hand with rebellion." She laughs, like she got me there, but she's wrong.

She's wrong.

"Like you said, there's the rock image, and I'm sure many bands indulge in it to the hilt. But what if they don't follow that image? What if they work together because they care about each other, not to mention they love the music? What if they don't indulge in excess, and that's why they've been around so long? Wouldn't that be the real rebellion right there? Going against what's expected of them?"

"So you mean to tell me your father's band, of all the rock bands ever known to the music world, is the only band to ever behave responsibly for the sake of the child in tow?"

"What I'm saying," *you annoying bitch,* "is if they acted irresponsibly, they never did it in front of me. Those guys are my family, okay? They have families too. They're fathers and husbands, good, loving people. I don't know where you get this negative idea that they're dimwits incapable of raising children."

"I never said that. I know you're too young to understand where I'm coming from. But your mother, for example—"

"My mother," I interrupt, because if she even tries, *tries* to disrespect my mother, I will personally slap her right here, right now, and get it all on tape, "is my hero, okay?"

Did I just say that? I feel a big-ass smile creeping up, but I hold it back, or she won't believe a word of this. I hardly believe I'm saying it myself. But it's true. My mom could've left too, after what Dad did to her, but she didn't. She stayed. To try and work things out.

"She was a working woman before I was born and a working woman afterward. Why should she have to change that because I came into the picture? Yeah, so she got pregnant before she wanted to. But she had a tough decision to make. Should she stay home and take care of me while my dad went on tour, but then I'd never see my dad? Or should she take me along, so I'd have them both and maybe learn about the world firsthand instead of by reading textbooks at home?"

"Desert." She sighs. "You're still young. I know you can't see the implications yet."

"No, you're wrong! I do understand! I'm sixteen—not six! I understand that you're incapable of seeing this any other way. A loving home environment for your kids can be made anywhere . . . anywhere! I don't mean to sound all sixties and whatever, but all a baby needs to be happy is love. I mean, hello?" Is this not obvious? Duh!

Adriana keeps listening, her silence prompting me to go on.

"My parents love me," I add. "Does it matter if I saw that love at Orly Airport in Paris, or in a playpen backstage at Madison Square Garden? So what? As long as we're together as a family, isn't that a basic unit right there? Why can't you just understand that?"

She doesn't even have to agree, just respect that my mom chose to do things differently from her. And I'm glad she did now. I'm glad.

Adriana reaches over her notes to the tape recorder on the table. She clicks it off. She could go on. She could ask more questions, backing off at nothing, until she gets what she wants. But she doesn't.

"This isn't necessary, Desert. You've made your point, sweetie. You can go." Then a smile.

"That's it?"

"That's it."

"Why? What about the rest of the interview?" I ask.

"*Mamita*, do you care for Liam?"

Liam? This is about Liam?

"Well, yeah! What's not to care for?" I say. He's my friend, he's helped me see things about myself, he's a super-incredible guy. I mean, please!

"Then we won't do this. He didn't want it anyway. Go home, mama."

"But—"

"Before I turn this back on," she says, reaching for her tape recorder.

I grab my bag and bolt for the door. But on my way out, I realize something else. Adriana's all right. Maybe her perspective was a little off, that's all.

"Thanks," I tell her, and she responds with a nod and a slow blink.

Outside the door, I let loose my big-ass smile.

Chapter Twenty-Nine

"What was that for?" Mom asks, bewildered by my impromptu bear hug. She's at her desk, a huge paper mess everywhere. Pen over her ear. Frazzled, working, solving Mom. Beautiful. Just beautiful.

"Nothing," I say, but my heart feels full.

Everything. You're the best.

Outside the office Faith is coming down the stairs, tight pants, platform shoes, hair carefully misplaced, makeup on, all but the big red nose. Behind her, some dude carrying her bags. Packed and out of here.

"Shut up, okay?" she says, slipping on her sunglasses.

How classy. "I wasn't saying anything."

"Right. Desert without any comments. Uh-huh."

Whatever. I swear, the only thing missing from this picture is the little poodle on a gold leash. The baggage dude opens the front door with his pinky, Faith mumbles something that sounds like, "Good luck without me, geezers," and the whole clown show exits.

Party!

With Faith gone now, Dad's going to be even busier than before. He'll start writing new songs soon, new lyrics. It'll be sort of like starting all over again. J. C., Max, and Phil are coming over later tonight. That's a good sign. I don't know why, but I'm really excited about this. Excited to have them over, having the family around all over again, to work with Dad, keeping him busy, doing what they do. It's like the old days, the pre-Faith days.

Sunday night. Sigh. I haven't stopped thinking about my family, Liam, Becca, Adriana, everything. It's been wild. Weird, wild, wacky stuff. I have to turn in a book report to Ms. Smigla by tomorrow, and I haven't even finished half of it. It's not like nobody knows how *Romeo and Juliet* ends or anything. How it ends, geez. That could've been Becca.

I open my notebook. All my work is in careful order, from the very first day. All my homework assignments graded and returned. A. A. A. A+. A++. A+++. Smig is so dramatic. Especially with the poems. I guess Dad has a point. I don't really have any hobbies, and while I do appreciate music intensely, and can even play some, writing is my thing.

Writing is my thing. I just realized that right now. Who would've guessed?

I make fun of Dad, and don't get me wrong, I'll make fun of him till the day I die, because he's my dad, and dads are perfect targets, even if they happen to be Flesh. But as much as I might make fun of him for the way he bares his soul to the world, I know a truth, and he knows it too. A truth we don't talk about much. One that I've only started to realize, but don't even want to admit sometimes.

That I'm him. I'm basically him, about twenty-three years younger. We may be very different in loads of ways, but writing connects us. These poems, this one about the water, and this one, the park, and this one. I leaf through my pages. Now I know how Dad felt. And to think I actually accused him once of being overly dramatic, writing all kinds of sappy stuff just for a reaction, just for the listener's approval. But I know it wasn't like that. I know it, now. He did it because he had to, because it was a need to get it out of his head, or else he'd lose it.

A need.

water is pure, day is clear
Thoughts purge, release all fear
Fog lifts off a cluttered mind

clouds break slow, I can see
Many roads ahead of me
Take this and use it as I wish

211

Fog has lifted, the cluttered mind
Rain is gone, storms unkind
Soon I will be gone again
Soon I will be gone

Dad's alone. As usual. Working, thinking, aching. I know he's aching because he's writing. His pencil scurries across the page, scratching at the paper. I know he's deep in thought because he doesn't hear me when I walk into the studio. Writing is painful, and risky. And he does it, still he does it, for everyone to see and hear.

"Dad." A whisper.

His face lifts from his pensive pose, turns to see me. He smiles. He always smiles when he sees me. I love that about him. "Girly."

Girly. Such a silly little name can lift my heart. Especially now.

"What're you doing?" I ask, because it's what I always ask. Even though nothing changes. My dad is doing what he always does, what he does best.

He sighs. "What do you think?"

"It's easier, though, right? Writing without Faith here?"

"Yeah." He breathes. "Actually, it is. I really don't care anymore, Des. I can't use her stuff. It's not that there's anything wrong with it. I'm sure she does really well and I wish her luck, but it's just not me." He shakes his head, looking down at his work again.

"I know." Dad could never be Faith. Thank God for that! He is so much more. Dimensions and light-years and all that more.

For a while we're quiet. I love how I can interrupt my dad while he's writing, and he's okay with it. Anybody else interrupts him, and they'll have hell to pay. But he's fine with me there, and I never get the sense he wants me out. It's like I'm another layer of him, standing there, watching over him. And he knows it.

"Dad?"

"Yeah, baby," he answers, crossing out in a graphite cloud the words he can't seem to make clear.

"I know the whole thing with Faith was so the twenty-five-and-unders could identify with the music."

He doesn't look up. Just keeps writing. "Something like that, Des. It doesn't matter anymore. If they can't connect with my lyrics, that's nobody's fault." Then he eyes me in that way he does when he really wants me to understand something. "Either they enjoy them, or they don't. I can't ask for anything more. We have to get back to what counts, the music, clicking, enjoying it for what it is, while we're still together. If nobody buys into it, that's their problem. I'll still be at peace."

Yes. He's right. I totally get it.

"Still," I say, "it'd be good to have some songs that young people can relate to, even if it's just to get them to buy the CD, so they can hear the better songs, right? Like getting a foot in the door?"

"Yeah, that's true, girly. You got it."

"So . . ." God, I am crazy for doing this. So freakin' crazy. "I don't know what good this does, or if you can even use any of this crap, but here's some stuff I wrote."

His expression changes, pauses. He looks at me, trying to see me differently. "What stuff, hon?"

If I hand him these sheets, it's all over. My private thoughts will end up in CD racks, cars, players, people's minds everywhere. But I don't care anymore. I kind of need for it to be out there.

"Well, the bracket you're targeting, the twenty-five-and-unders, I think maybe they can relate to this. I mean, it's all teen angst anyway," I say, handing him my poems. He reaches for them, fingertips closing over the sheets softly.

Let go, Des. Let go. You can do it, girly.

I release my grip, and he begins to scan over them. I watch his expression, changing from faint smile to recognition, to guilt maybe, to connection. I can tell he's connected with something, some words I wrote. He's nodding.

"Girly," he says with a smile. "This is wonderful."

He loves them. The Almighty Flesh loves my poems! I don't know why that surprises me. I mean, I've always known that my dad likes my writing, but still, this confirms it right here. I always kind of thought that maybe he was just saying it to encourage me, you know, like any parent should encourage the twinkling of a talent, but no.

Then his smile dampens. "Wonderful. But personal. I can't use them, hon. Believe me, it means everything to me that you're offering them, and I know how hard it must be for you to be doing this . . . but I have to write my own. You know, it's—"

"A need. I know, Dad." Whew, this is kind of a relief!

He looks down at them again, rereading. "They are beautiful, though, Des. Absolutely beautiful. You are so gifted, you know that?" He shakes his head like he can't believe I wrote them.

"Dad, come on, all parents think that."

"No, really. Truly, Desert. This," he says, shuffling the sheets one behind the other, taking another look at the lines, "this is talent, hon. This makes me look bad. I have no doubt whatsoever that these words'll be seen by millions of people someday. Whether you write songs or not." He reaches for my hand and gives it a squeeze. "Thanks, girly, but save 'em. You'll use 'em one day."

Something in my heart breaks just then. I can't explain it. I can feel my father's acceptance. Acceptance that the time's coming when he'll need to let someone else be heard, someone with his voice, but different. Female maybe, twenty-three years younger, a different perspective, and yet the same.

I have no doubt that someone will be me.

And that means . . . I am in such deep shit, now. The world is gonna see these. My inner thoughts. Maybe not right away, but . . . holy crappy poems, Batman!

"Hey Dad," I say. "Write whatever it takes to keep you guys going, okay?"

And if I have to tour along for another seventeen years, so be it. I'm fine with that.

That's been my life in a nutshell anyway.

Chapter Thirty

Why can't I take Moonlit Park with me? All these trees. This bench. Wrap them up and stuff them into the trucks. And Liam. I can smuggle Liam on bus two as a roadie. Now *that* would be a killer story for Adriana.

"At least you made it through one, whole school year." Liam tries to make me feel better.

I grin and nod but can't speak. I'm going to miss this boy. I mean, really miss him.

"What am I supposed to do without you for five months?" he asks, holding my waist with one hand and sliding his other along my ponytail.

"I dunno. Think of me?" I tilt my face up and stare into those baby blues. He's killing me. *Take a mental picture of him, Desert.*

Freeze it. Just like that.

"What if I wanna fly in to a show and surprise you? Will I find you with someone else?"

Right! "Not unless he's your long-lost twin who came to surprise me first!"

He smiles and leans down to kiss me. I have to make this one last. . . .

The next day Becca stands there, watching the crew load bus one. It's rumbling and hissing, and I never realize how much I miss the smell of bus exhaust until we start a new tour. I know, I know . . . weird. And Becca looks like she wants to tag along too.

"I said good-bye to him last night." I grab my pillow from a stack of suitcases. "Believe me, it wasn't easy."

"I'll keep an eye on him for you," she says, pushing her hair behind her ears.

"That's okay. We agreed to stay friends. I can't ask him to wait for me while I'm gone, Beck. If he's not with someone else by the time I get back, then maybe we'll hook up again. But I do love him. I told him that."

She smiles her sad smile and looks away.

"Oh! I can't believe I almost forgot."

"What?" she says.

"Here, hold this a second." I give her my backpack, my pillow, and my iPod. I run off to bus two and pull a flight case out of the luggage compartment.

Becca sees me coming back and smiles . . . none of that sorry, pained stuff but a real, big grin across her face.

I stand the guitar case on its edge in front of her. "J. C. left early this morning," I say. "He said to give you this. It's a Martin. Don't ask me which model."

Her eyes totally light up as she opens the latches to take a peek inside. "You've got to be kidding me!"

"I kid you not. It's yours."

She stands and rings her arm around me, pressing her cheek against mine, almost dropping my player in the process. "Thank you *so* much! I can't believe him! Tell him I say thanks!"

"I'll do that." I love seeing her get all goofy like a little kid.

"So the last show is in Miami?" She lets go and hands me back my stuff.

"Yep. November tenth."

"Well, then . . . I guess we'll see you there." She smirks kind of awkward, and I know what she means. This is the real good-bye now. Becca's eyes are all shiny.

Augh! I hate this. "Hey, stop it. I'll be back. And I'll be calling and e-mailing you guys all the time. Trust me." I pull out an envelope from my backpack's outer pocket and hand it to her.

"What's this?" she asks, flipping it over in her hands.

"For the Miami show. For you and Liam. Two backstage passes."

She nods, and we hug real hard for the last time. I turn around and step onto the bus. At the top step I look at Becca again, her rotten sneakers, the guitar at her feet. "Later."

She flashes me a peace sign.

DATE DUE

GAYLORD   #3523PI   Printed in USA